"You've...been ... tell me you we...

"I had the time," Katrien said, not knowing how to deal with this. She looked away, clasped and unclasped her hands, and finally said, "I wanted to help."

"I'm...grateful." Zachary paused, took a couple of labored breaths. "Only a bit...confused."

"Yes, I—" Where did she start explaining?

"Must be the...hypothermia." He drew a struggling breath. "Along with...everything else...seem to be suffering...a bit of amnesia. I love you, Katrien...but...when did we get engaged?"

DAPHNE CLAIR lives in subtropical New Zealand, with her Dutch-born husband. They have five children. At eight years old she embarked on her first novel, about taming a tiger. This epic never reached a publisher, but metamorphosed male tigers still prowl the pages of her romances. She has won literary prizes for short stories and nonfiction, and has also published poetry. As Laurey Bright she writes for Silhouette.

Daphne Clair

RECKLESS ENGAGEMENT

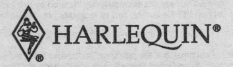

TORONTO • NEW YORK • LONDON
AMSTERDAM • PARIS • SYDNEY • HAMBURG
STOCKHOLM • ATHENS • TOKYO • MILAN • MADRID
PRAGUE • WARSAW • BUDAPEST • AUCKLAND

ISBN 0-373-18725-4

RECKLESS ENGAGEMENT

First North American Publication 2000.

Copyright © 1997 by Daphne de Jong.

This edition published by arrangement with Harlequin Books S.A.

® and TM are trademarks of the publisher. Trademarks indicated with ® are registered in the United States Patent and Trademark Office, the Canadian Trade Marks Office and in other countries.

Visit us at www.romance.net

Printed in U.S.A.

CHAPTER ONE

THE man of her dreams.

She knew him. Knew him in the abrupt tightness of her breath, and in the hot quicksilver that had suddenly replaced her bones, so that her body seemed held together by nothing but the startling tension that suffused it.

Across the big high-ceilinged room, filled with people holding glasses of wine and restlessly chattering, the man's head lifted as though he'd felt the concentration of her stare, and his eyes met hers.

A dark brow lifted in amused enquiry, and a hint of masculine speculation entered fathomless sea-green eyes. The hard lines of his mouth took on a subtle curve.

'Katie?' Callum touched Katrien's arm, and she flinched. 'Katie?'

Her eyes ached. She blinked, moistening them. 'Sorry. I was thinking.' Her fiancé's familiar features and perfectly groomed sandy hair, and the kind blue eyes peering worriedly into her clear silver-grey ones, seemed faraway, in another dimension.

The stranger's hair, almost as black as his decisive brows, was carelessly cut, showing a tendency to curl onto the collar of his dinner suit. He stood with a hand thrust into a trouser pocket, his stance one of casual ease, and yet he didn't seem to belong in this elegant gathering. Perhaps it was because he was so big—broad in the shoulders and tall.

'I'll get you a drink,' Callum offered, steering Katrien further into the crowd. He beckoned a passing waiter

and took two glasses from the silver tray the man prof-
fered. 'Here, you look as though you need it.' As her
hand closed about the glass, Callum worried, 'You
haven't really got over that flu, have you? You've lost
weight.' He touched a strand of the thick, russet-lit hair
that lay on her bared shoulders, and smoothed it back
from her cheek.

Katrien made her lips move into a smile. 'I'm fine,
really.' She took a sip of the wine, cool and dry to her
tongue. And smiled again. 'Models are supposed to be
thin.'

Callum smiled back, making an intimacy of it. 'I don't
want you *too* thin.' He raised his glass at her before
drinking from it. 'To us…our future.'

An inexplicable panic fluttered about her heart. Then
a couple they knew swooped on them, and while the
man clapped Callum on the shoulder the woman demanded to see her ring.

Katrien obligingly held out her left hand, regarding
the large diamond flanked by two smaller ones with dis-
turbing detachment, almost as though she hadn't been
there when Callum had plucked it from the jeweller's
tray and smoothed it onto her finger, declaring with sat-
isfaction that it fitted so perfectly it might have been
made for her.

She tried to recapture the glow of warmth that she'd
felt then, scarcely two weeks ago. Tried to fix her mind
on the conversation of her companions. But all the time
she was fighting an urge to look for the man who had
evoked that powerful sense of recognition when she'd
first entered.

Some inward antenna seemed to tell her when he
moved, coming closer. A shiver passed over her skin,
and she couldn't stop herself from turning her head,
hunting him down. He wasn't looking in her direction,

but at the touch of her gaze she saw his shoulders tauten, his head begin to swivel, and she forced herself to look away, fixing Callum with such an attentive look that he faltered in what he was saying and looked at her enquiringly.

Katrien gave him an encouraging smile, and drank some more of her wine. She hadn't the faintest idea what the topic of conversation was.

The man moved away, and now the crowd was drifting towards the tables in an adjoining room.

Callum took her emptied glass and deposited it with another waiter. She felt as though she was walking on a layer of fog between the high heels of her shoes and the floor. Maybe she had downed the wine too quickly on an empty stomach. Just as well they were to have dinner.

It was a charity affair in aid of the widow and children of a mountaineer who had died on a New Zealand expedition to the Himalayas some months ago, the after-dinner speech to be given by a friend who had survived the journey—Zachary Ballantine. There had been photographs of him in all the national papers at the time of the tragedy—grainy snapshots of a gaunt and bearded man with haunted dark eyes shadowed by snow-frosted brows under the fur-edged hood of his parka.

Every TV station and newspaper in New Zealand must have wanted his story, but he had shunned the news media, refusing to give interviews. Yet someone had persuaded him to speak tonight.

The man she found so unsettling was seated at a table near the shallow dais on which a microphone stood ready. Katrien looked at him once and then dragged her gaze away. She hardly tasted the food that was put before her, mechanically emptying the plates until she found herself staring at a mound of chocolate cake and cream, and her stomach revolted. She pushed away the dish and grabbed her wine glass. It was empty—again. She'd already drunk far more than usual, but when Callum refilled the glass she gave him a distracted smile and raised the glass to her lips.

His arm came around her, a hand squeezing her shoulder. 'Are you okay?' he whispered, glancing at her untouched dessert.

'Of course. You know I don't usually eat sweets, and anyway I'm full.'

He smiled and nuzzled her temple with his cheek. 'It'll do you good.' He drew back slightly and his gaze lingered on her bare shoulders and the low neckline of her dress. 'You can do with a bit more weight. Not that you aren't gorgeous.' His fingers tightened. 'I can't wait to get you alone.' Turning aside briefly, he took a spoon and scooped up some of the untouched dessert, presenting it to her with a teasing grin. 'Open up.'

Katrien laughed and shook her head, but he insisted, and she parted her lips and let him slide the spoonful between them. It tasted sickly, and when he repeated the gesture she put a staying hand on his wrist, smiling so that he wouldn't think she was angry. 'No, really. I can't eat any more.'

Callum was smiling too. 'You have a bit of cream...' He ducked his head and licked it from the corner of her mouth.

Someone across the table laughed, and Katrien drew back, turning away.

Her gaze collided with a stormy, deep green one across the room.

She felt heat along her cheekbones as the man's brooding expression changed to amusement tinged with satire. A faint anger stirred inside her, along with an odd recurrence of fear.

Callum said, 'I was only teasing—'

'I know.' She turned back to him. 'It's okay.' Callum was sensitive to her moods. It was one reason why she loved him.

Coffee was served and the chairwoman of the committee got up to introduce the guest speaker with a long spiel about his adventurous career climbing mountains, working in the Antarctic, helping to build a hospital in Nepal, and exploring the world's highest, wildest regions. She stepped down and led a round of introductory applause for Zachary Ballantine.

The lights dimmed except for the spotlight illuminating the dais. And with a curious lack of surprise Katrien watched the man who got up to walk forward with an unhurried, confident stride to take his place behind the microphone. Without the beard she hadn't recognised him earlier.

He looked around the room, and she thought his sea-coloured eyes flickered as they met hers; then he glanced at a card in his hand and began to speak.

Katrien stared at the cup of coffee before her, watched the steam rising from it, and picked up a spoon, then quietly replaced it in the saucer. She took her coffee black, no sugar.

He had a resonant voice like dark, slightly gritty honey. At the first syllable Katrien felt a profound sense of recognition, a reverberating bell note deep in her soul.

For a long time she just listened to the sound, not the words, fixing her gaze on the white tablecloth before her. But in the end her eyes lifted and found him where he stood on the raised dais, commanding the room. And as if he knew, his head tilted and he paused, his gaze momentarily homing in on her. He looked away and consulted the card in his hand again before shoving it into his pocket and continuing his speech.

She tried to curb the hurried rhythm of her heart, telling herself he could scarcely see anyone in the partially lit room.

Beside her Callum stirred, his fingers still resting lightly on her bare shoulder, and she fought an extraordinary urge to shrug away from his touch.

'There's no feeling quite like being literally on top of the world,' Zachary Ballantine was saying. 'Standing on the summit of Everest, looking down across those mountains, a view that goes on for ever—it puts all the pain, the effort, the danger into perspective. You know then that whatever you went through to get there, it was all worth it. Every climber wants to do Everest. Ben and I did it for the first time together—five years ago. It was something neither of us would ever forget.'

He paused again, staring at the floor as if searching it for inspiration. Someone clinked a coffee cup into its saucer. Someone else shuffled a chair.

Zachary Ballantine looked up slowly. 'After that, all you can do is search for harder climbs, untried routes, more challenges, mountains that are still unconquered.'

'Why?' Callum muttered humorously in Katrien's ear.

Katrien shook her head slightly. She didn't understand either, but suddenly, passionately, she wanted to. She was concentrating now, intently, afraid to miss a word.

'There's always another mountain.' The man in the circle of light placed a hand on the gleaming chrome of the microphone stand and gripped it. 'Always another challenge, another risk, another Circe luring men to lay down their lives for her...'

His voice had lowered and he was staring at his hand clasped about the cold metal rod before him. This time when he stopped speaking no whisper of sound touched the silence.

Katrien was sure that for a second or two he had forgotten his audience and departed from his prepared script. He released his hold and thrust his hand into his pocket.

'Men,' he said slowly, his gaze seemingly fixed on some distant point outside the room, 'and women, make mistakes. And the mountains are unforgiving. Last year they took the closest friend I've ever had—or ever will have. Ben Storey was the best.' His head turned slightly and his eyes shifted and refocused to meet Katrien's. She felt her own head lift infinitesimally, her gaze caught by the naked pain in his. 'The best friend, the best mountain man, the greatest person I've ever known. I miss him.'

He stepped back then one pace, out of the brightness of the light. His pain crashed around her, and she closed her eyes against it, her body trembling, her throat aching with the effort not to cry.

When she opened her eyes he was gone, taking his seat again amidst a wave of applause. Callum had removed his clasp from her shoulder to join in the clapping, and she wrenched apart the hands locked damply in her lap and did the same.

A woman across the table picked up her napkin and wiped away a tear.

I'm not the only one, Katrien told herself. He probably had the same effect on every woman in the room.

The purpose of the evening was to raise funds for the dead mountaineer's family. Zachary Ballantine's speech had been calculated to arouse sympathy. And no doubt he had been genuinely fond of his friend. It was very sad but she knew neither of them, and when the news had first broken of the disastrous expedition her chief emotions had been pity for the woman who had lost her husband and the father of her two children, and a sort of distant anger with the man who had deliberately put his life in danger despite their dependence on him.

She had never understood what drove anyone to take

insane risks in order to experience some adrenalin high
that apparently came with the knowledge that death was
breathing down one's neck. It seemed to her a bizarre,
aberrant way of living.

Watching Zachary Ballantine rise to shake hands with
a pretty young woman who had rushed to his table and
now gazed at him with something approaching adora-
tion, Katrien was unexpectedly angry all over again.
How could they—men like him, with grace and attraction and the glamour that clung to them as known ad-
venturers—make women love them, and then carelessly
throw away their lives in pursuit of some *Boys' Own*
dream? It was unfair, and downright cruel.

The young woman smiled and touched his arm, her
white, ringless hand resting on the sleeve of his jacket,
her lovely face earnest as she spoke to him, no doubt
artlessly telling of her admiration, leaving herself open
to being hurt by him.

'You fool.' Katrien's lips shaped the words.

'What?' Callum leaned closer.

She shook her head. 'Nothing. Can we go now?' She
didn't think she could bear watching this any longer. Her
emotions seemed to have turned into some ill-tempered
steed, bucking and swerving all over the place. Maybe
Callum was right; she hadn't fully recovered from the
bout of flu that had recently attacked her.

'You don't want to speak to the guest of honour first?'
Callum enquired.

There was a bevy of people around him now. The girl
was standing on the outskirts, looking slightly crest-
fallen. 'No,' Katrien said. 'He has plenty of admirers.
And I'm...tired.'

Callum gave a surprised grin at the unintended wasp-
ishness in her tone. He stood up to pull out her chair.
'Come on, then. I'll get us a cab.' He never drove his

car if he was going to be drinking. Callum's strict sense
of responsibility was another of the things she liked
about him. He would never worry her by going off on
some wild, hazardous adventure.

He left her standing in the carpeted foyer, a light
woollen wrap draped about her shoulders, while he ventured into the street to find a taxi.

She shouldn't have drunk so much. Her head felt
weightless and a bit swimmy. Shifting from foot to foot,
she looked around for a chair. The only two—gilt affairs
flanking a tiny marble-topped table—were occupied by
a couple having a low-voiced but apparently passionate
conversation.

Closing her eyes, she leaned back against the em-
bossed paper on the wall.

'Are you all right?'

Recognising the deep voice, Katrien straightened with
a jerk, her eyes flying wide. Black spots danced before
her vision and her forehead went cold and damp.

Hard hands clamped on her arms, steadying her. She
ducked her head and closed her eyes again, willing away
the brief dizziness before slowly and carefully looking
up.

So near, Zachary Ballantine's sea-green eyes were un-
comfortably penetrating. She could see the lift of his
cheekbones beneath faintly tanned skin, and a tiny white
scar at the corner of his upper lip; smell soap, and wool
suiting and a hint of something that brought to mind pine
trees and wooded, snowy slopes. Aftershave?

She said, 'Yes, I'm all right. Thank you.'

He still held her arms. 'You're very pale.'

'I've had the flu.' His grasp was less tight now, his
thumbs making absent stroking movements against her
skin. Katrien's breath clutched at her throat, and she

swallowed. 'You're not leaving?' she asked him. There must still be dozens of people wanting to speak to him.

'I was on my way to the men's room,' he said, 'when I saw you alone and palely loitering...' He smiled. 'I thought you were about to faint.'

No man should have a smile like that. It was positively lethal, glinting in his eyes and tilting the masculine planes of his mouth into a seductive curve framing a glimpse of white, even teeth.

She felt the involuntary tightening of her facial muscles, the widening of her eyes. And knew he'd read the startling, inappropriate quickening of sexual awareness when his own eyes darkened and the smile died from his mouth. She saw the slight flare of his nostrils as he took a deeper breath, and long dark lashes momentarily veiled his eyes as he dropped his gaze a few inches to her parted lips.

Katrien felt dizzy again, and perhaps he noticed, because his hold on her arms became more urgent, almost painful.

Her body curved towards him, her spine arching subtly, her head tipping back—movements that were small but unmistakable. Her eyelids fluttered, and she watched his mouth part as he leaned towards her.

Then Callum's voice said, 'Okay, Katie—got one.' And, more sharply, 'What's going on?'

Katrien jumped, automatically raising her hands to push ineffectually at Zachary Ballantine's chest as her body stiffened.

His hands slid from her arms without haste and he turned. 'Who are you?' he demanded of the man who had been at Katrien's side all evening and was now striding towards them.

Callum blinked, looking both outraged and uncertain. Katrien laid a hand on his arm as she stepped to his side. 'This is Callum Steward,' she said. 'My fiancé. Mr Ballantine thought I was going to faint, Callum,' she explained. 'He was kind enough to stop and...offer his help.'

Her cheeks burned. She knew that her fiancé's searching glance would see no sign of paleness now.

Callum's arm slipped about her waist. 'You felt faint?'

'Just a bit. I'm all right now.' She risked a fleeting glance at Zachary Ballantine, and saw that he appeared cynically amused.

Addressing Callum, he said, 'I wouldn't leave her alone if I were you.' As she looked up again his eyes shifted, giving her a cool, assessing stare. 'She seems likely to fall into the arms of any passing stranger.'

Katrien sucked in a choking breath. 'Not at all. It was a momentary dizziness. I'm sure it would have passed.'

'Apparently,' Zachary Ballantine observed, 'it has.'

'Still,' Callum said with a shade too much heartiness, 'I'm grateful you were there to catch her, Mr Ballantine. We enjoyed your talk, by the way.' He held out his hand, and after a moment the big man took it in his.

'Thank you.'

'Thank *you* for looking after my fiancée. Now if you'll excuse us, I've got a cab outside. Come on, darling...'

As they walked away and Callum pushed open the door, ushering her into the wintry air outside, Katrien knew that the other man was watching them. She resisted turning to look back at him.

Zachary Ballantine was the stuff dreams were made of. Every woman's fantasy. His friend who had died on the mountain had been another one. She recalled a picture of Ben Storey published in the aftermath of his death—a young god smiling against the backdrop of a snow-covered mountain, the sun glinting on his golden hair, the hood of his parka pushed back and a pair of goggles slung about his neck.

On the same page had been a picture of his widow, looking with tearless bravery straight into the camera as she cradled the youngest of her children in her arms while the other leaned against her knee.

Katrien even remembered the caption: 'Mountaineer "died doing what he wanted".' The quote had been from Wendy Storey, the woman who had supported his insane aspirations and borne his children. Like everyone else she had praised his courage. Katrien had admired hers more.

'Thank heaven,' she said to Callum as he got into the cab beside her and took her hand in his, 'you have no desire to conquer mountains.'

'How do you know?' he asked her lightly.

Katrien directed him a look of undiluted horror.

Callum laughed, pulling her into his arms. 'I have other desires,' he growled in her ear.

She let him kiss her, and kissed him back, trying to banish from behind her closed lids the vivid memory of aroused male curiosity in a pair of deep green eyes.

When the taxi driver let them out at the door of her flat in the inner suburb of Herne Bay, her hair had lost its sleek styling and Callum was breathing less than evenly. He fumbled as he dug in his wallet for money to pay the driver before following Katrien inside.

She made coffee and they sat side by side on the comfortable softness of the two-seater sofa in her sitting room while they drank it, but when he took her in his arms again she laid her head on his shoulder and said, 'I'm really tired, Callum.'

He stroked her hair. 'I'm a selfish brute.'

'No, you're not. You're the nicest man I've ever

known. But I guess you're right…I haven't quite got over the flu bug. I'm sorry.'

'Don't worry about it.' He kissed her forehead. 'I'll wait until you're properly well again.'

He *was* the nicest man she knew. So why was she suddenly finding it impossible to look at him? Why did she feel that if he didn't leave soon she'd scream?

She kissed him on the lips, not giving him a chance to reciprocate before she pulled away and turned to rise from the sofa and pick up their cups. 'Maybe next time…' she muttered vaguely.

Almost any other man would have swept her into bed the minute he'd got a ring on her finger, if not before. Callum had too much finesse for that. He'd been prepared to wait for the right moment. And when the right moment was delayed by her inconveniently succumbing to the nasty ailment that seemed to have afflicted half the population this winter, he'd sent her flowers and phoned every day, even called in person with offers of nursing and food.

She'd wanted only to be left alone to subsist on packet soups and orange juice, and not to have him see her looking and feeling like a sodden and aching dishrag.

His offers spurned, Callum had phoned her sister, and Miranda had come round regularly with chicken soup and aspirin and bracing sympathy, sometimes bringing the youngest of her three children, with strict instructions to stay out of the sickroom and not disturb Aunty Kat.

Callum phoned for another cab while Katrien took the cups into the kitchen. She fussed around washing and drying them and putting away the sugar bowl she'd taken out for Callum's coffee, making sure that no grains had spilled on the bench to attract Auckland's voracious ants. Of course there were none. If there had been Callum would have wiped them up himself.

She was hanging up the tea towel when he came to the kitchen doorway. 'I'll be off, then,' he said. 'The cab will be here in a few minutes.'

She walked with him to the door, and he kissed her gently and lingeringly, his thumbs stroking her cheeks as he lifted his head and smiled down at her.

She recalled Zachary Ballantine caressing her arms. His skin had been less smooth than Callum's, the pads of his thumbs faintly rasping.

She closed the door behind Callum and leaned against it, her forehead on the painted wood. What was wrong with her tonight?

She had a warm shower, then climbed into bed wearing a fleecy-lined cotton nightshirt. After switching off the light she lay staring into the darkness for a long time.

When at last her eyes drifted shut and the night enfolded her, he came.

It was the same as always. The man held her in his strong, imprisoning arms, and spoke words she couldn't hear. And she struggled, frightened and unable to breathe, trapped in silent, murky depths, until the dark voice commanded her stillness, her compliance. And the words came clearly to her—*Trust me*.

The voice changed to reassurance, soothing her panic away. She felt his mouth on her lips, his breath filling her, the warmth of his body against the utter coldness of hers. And then the warmth flooded her as she clung to him while he lifted her and carried her out of the blackness and into the dazzle of light. And she opened her closed eyes and looked up at him.

She had dreamed of him so often that she knew now how the bright sun behind him shadowed his features, so that she could never see what he looked like.

Only this time it was different. His eyes were the deep green of the sea, and his hair was sleeked back but stubbornly waved; the chest she rested against and his shoulders under her encircling arms were bare and muscled.

He looked at her and smiled, and she felt her lips part under the lambent fire in his gaze.

Then he lowered his head and at the touch of his mouth on hers, her eyes flew open on darkness.

Her heart pounded as if she'd been running, and the bedclothes were disarrayed about her heated body. She pulled at them, then sat up and switched the bedside lamp back on, pushed back tumbled hair from her damp temples and squinted down at the time on her watch.

She'd been asleep for less than an hour.

Slumping back on the pillows, she left the light on and fiercely gazed at the cream-painted wall opposite her bed.

She had *never* been able to see the man. Sometimes she'd woken crying with frustration because he wouldn't reveal himself to her, wouldn't let her find out what he looked like.

Now, for the first time, the man of her dreams—and nightmares—had a face.

CHAPTER TWO

'YOU know I don't do swimsuit work.' Katrien handed back the folder her agent had passed to her.

Hattie Fisher sighed. 'You're limiting your options. And this assignment—'

'Yes, the money's good.'

'The advertising agency asked for you specially, you know.'

'I'm flattered that they want me, but I'll pass on this one, thanks.'

'I don't have anything else for you at the moment, until that shampoo commercial you're booked for.'

'That's okay. I could do with a break.' Katrien quashed a tremor of anxiety. She'd had to pull out of her last assignment when she got the flu and now here she was with only one confirmed booking in view. Modelling work within New Zealand was limited, and although in the past she'd flown to Australia at the drop of a hat, and sometimes further afield, she'd promised Callum to limit her overseas assignments. But she had her savings, and maybe it was time she took a holiday.

'Skiing?' Callum looked doubtful, stirring sugar into his coffee. Katrien had phoned his office and suggested meeting for lunch at their favourite downtown café. 'Do you think that's wise when you're just getting over the flu?'

'Mountain air's healthy, they say. And there's a special deal going at Whakapapa, with accommodation at the Chateau.'

'Well, at least you'd be comfortable, in a decent hotel.'

More than decent, Katrien thought. The wonderful old hotel offered luxury on the ski fields. 'With all the rumbling Mount Ruapehu's been doing in the last couple of seasons, I guess they have to get as many people down there as they can.' The volcano had created havoc by spreading ash on the snow and many tourists had been frightened away by the danger of eruptions, although others had enjoyed the thrill of watching the mountain throw fire and rocks into the sky. The ski fields had not opened on schedule and the operators had lost a lot of money.

'You'll get cold and wet,' Callum fussed. 'Suppose you have a relapse?'

'I'll be careful, and with the proper gear I won't get cold—or wet.'

'I wish I could come with you, but the bank wouldn't look kindly on a request for leave right now.' He was a senior bank executive and his job was much too important for him to go on holiday at a moment's notice.

'I wish you could come too,' Katrien assured him, disturbed to find that it was a lie. 'But you don't ski, and it's only for a week. You'll hardly know I'm gone.'

'Not true. I'll miss you every day.'

Katrien gave him an absent smile. 'That's sweet. I'll miss you too.' Surely it was the aftermath of her illness that had caused this odd lethargy of her emotions. When she was really over it the warm, loving feelings would come back. She reached out for his hand and his fingers closed around hers. 'I love you,' she murmured.

His clasp tightened and a flush came into his cheeks. He raised her hand to his face and pressed his lips into her palm. His voice muffled, he said, 'And I love you!'

Her heart contracted, shrinking. Gooseflesh chilled her

arms. She looked away, and was relieved when Callum lowered their joined hands to the table. Feeling guilty and bothered, she let her fingers lie slackly in his grasp. 'I've already made a booking,' she told him. 'I leave tomorrow morning.'

'That…' He cleared his throat. 'That was quick.'

'Once I'd made up my mind—' Katrien shrugged.

'Yes, well… You'll be packing tonight, then?'

Katrien forced herself to look at him regretfully, apologetically. 'I've got a lot to do.'

'When you get back…' Callum smiled hopefully.

'I'll be fully recovered then,' she promised. 'As soon as I'm home I'll let you know.'

The ski slopes were magnificent, the snow glinting like spun sugar in the wintry sun. Tiny figures zigzagged down the mountain, far below the adzed peaks veiled in snow and a drift of lazy cloud.

Looking forward to joining them, Katrien idled up the slope in the chairlift, the cold air numbing her nose even as the sun warmed her cheeks. She raised her eyes to the mountain top, and found herself speculating on what drove men like Zachary Ballantine. Going up with the object of skiing down again with the wind in her face and the snow sliding away beneath her skis was one thing. Climbing laboriously over sheer rock faces and across treacherous ice fields and skirting hidden crevasses with the sole aim of reaching the top was another, totally alien concept.

Her first skiing lesson had been during a photo shoot for a travel magazine. She'd been playing the part of a beginner—and played it convincingly because she was. Later she'd paid for more lessons, partly because she'd found it enjoyable and a challenge, and partly because she figured it might be a useful skill to add to her portfolio, just as it was handy to be able to sit on a horse without falling off. It had paid off. She'd gained a couple of assignments modelling winter sportswear on the strength of her ability to provide genuine action shots on skis.

The chairlift deposited her at the intermediate slope, a level at which she was quite confident now.

The snow was already crisscrossed with the marks of those who had gone before her. As she adjusted her goggles and took off, someone far below in a red jacket wavered, fell and landed in a flurry of snow, then picked themselves up again. The snow swished under her skis as she gathered momentum, her knees bent, her body perfectly balanced, the stretchy fabric of her bright pink body-hugging ski pants allowing her freedom of movement.

By the time she'd made the run a few times she was exhilarated. She'd taken a tumble once but had landed unhurt and untangled herself to complete the course with ease. The rest of the time she'd skied smoothly and well.

On her last run of the day down the milky incline, she saw a blur of dark blue and bright yellow to one side as another skier swooped past.

A man, slim-hipped, broad-shouldered, and skiing with such speed and grace that she couldn't help but admire his style. Surely he belonged on the uppermost slopes where the real experts hung out.

When she reached the end of the run she found herself looking around for him, but there was no blue and yellow ski suit in sight. She caught a bus back to the hotel and had an early meal and a leisurely hot soak, gave her skin a thorough moisturising treatment to combat the effects of sun and wind, and retired to her bed with a book, later slipping into a dreamless sleep.

The next day she decided to go to the third level and

think about testing herself out on it. If the run looked too difficult on close inspection she could ride down again to the familiar, less difficult slopes.

The summit appeared much nearer from where the chairlift left her this time. Today no cloud obscured the peak, and there was no sign of its recent volcanic activity. It looked remote and beautiful and unattainable. She remembered that in Maori legend the mountain was a woman, squabbled over by her jealous lovers, the other mountains nearby. One, Taranaki, had retired in dudgeon to the coast and now reigned there in splendid isolation. His rival Tongariro remained nearby, occasionally huffing and puffing his displeasure in clouds of volcanic steam.

Katrien watched a couple of skiers take off and gather speed while she stood by, still a little uncertain.

Deciding to have a cup of coffee first, she turned away from the ski field to the nearby café, leaving her skis with all the others leaning against the building before going in.

She was sipping coffee and contemplating the ski run when she heard the voice. 'Thanks a lot.'

That was all, but it brought her head whipping round, in time to see the back of a blue-and-yellow-clad figure disappear through the doorway. Tall, dark-haired.

No, she told herself. You're imagining things.

But she had hastily clattered her half-finished cup of coffee back into its saucer and was on her way to the door before she even realised what she was doing.

She'd look silly retracing her steps, so she kept walking out onto the deck.

He was bent over, doing up the buckles on his boots. She watched fatalistically until he'd straightened. And then he looked up and saw her.

'Mr Ballantine,' she said.

His surprise showed only in a faint lifting of his brows, an even fainter glint of light in his eyes. 'Hello,' he said, '...Katie.'

'It's Katrien,' she told him. 'Katrien Cromwell.'

He nodded. 'Katrien.' The name left his tongue like a caress, giving the 'r' a slight burr so that it sounded exotic and foreign.

'I saw you yesterday,' she told him, 'on the intermediate slope, but you seemed too good to be on that level.'

'I did a cross-country run yesterday, then made my way down the mountain.'

'I guess you have a lot of experience.'

Something changed in his eyes. He looked at her, standing there in her pink ski suit, her hair loose about her shoulders since she'd pulled off her hat when she entered the café. 'Some. How about you?' he asked.

Katrien wrenched her eyes from his and looked down the slope. 'I came up here today thinking I might try this run but...I'm not sure I'm quite brave enough.'

'Is your fiancé with you?'

She had to look back at him then. 'He wasn't able to get away. And anyway, he doesn't ski.'

His mouth tilted up at one corner and he gave a brief nod. 'I see.' There was a small silence. 'If you like, I'll go down with you.'

'I wouldn't like to hold you up. I don't suppose you want to spend your time nursing along a bunny skier.'

'You're no bunny,' he argued. 'You looked pretty competent yesterday.' At her surprised look, he added, 'I recognise the...outfit.' He cast a glance over the figure-hugging stretch pants and the fleecy-lined shirt under her open jacket. 'So...shall we go?'

It was a challenge, pure and simple. He waited for her to make up her mind whether to accept it, or to walk away and return to the less exciting lower slopes.

She stepped onto the snow and retrieved her skis.

The sound of their skis gliding on the slick white surface was like tearing silk. Katrien's hair streamed behind her, the momentum of her downhill flight dragging it back from her face. She had left the café in such a hurry she'd forgotten to retrieve her woollen hat.

Zachary was a blur of blue and yellow at her peripheral vision, a couple of times swooping away in a half loop, then coming back to stay at her side, moderating his speed to hers.

'Okay?' he shouted at her once, and she risked a look at his face, saw his white smile, and smiled back.

'Okay!'

When they reached the end of the run she fluffed the stop and ended up in a jumbled heap, laughing.

Zachary offered a gloved hand and helped her up. 'How was it?'

'Wonderful!' She brushed snow from her arms and body, and he reached out to flick away flakes of white from her hair.

His hand touched her cheek, and even though he still wore gloves, she felt a tingling awareness that stopped her smile and made her veil her eyes with her lashes. A flash of unease assailed her, and she tried to step away, forgetting she was wearing skis.

She would have toppled again if he hadn't caught at her arms. 'Steady.'

'Thanks.' She was breathless, not only from the run. 'And thanks for bringing me down. I might have chickened out otherwise.'

'I don't think so.'

She glanced up and into his eyes, uncertain what it was she read there.

Then he looked away up the slope and said, 'Want to try again?'

Why not? After the thrill of that descent, the thought of returning to the easier slopes seemed very tame. She nodded. 'Yes. But this time you don't need to wait for me.'

They shared a T-bar back to the top, holding on and standing side by side while little puffs of their steamy breath mingled in the frosty air.

Zachary waited for her to go first. She was halfway to the bottom when she heard a shout from behind and then two young men, whooping in feigned panic, went flying past, much too close for comfort. A quick look sideways showed her a third, about to cannon into her. She took evasive action and he careered on down the slope, but Katrien lost control and went sliding and skidding to the edge of the run, hitting her head painfully on a hidden rock under the snow and landing in a tangle of skis and poles, one of which went flying from her hand.

'Katrien!' Zachary slid to a stop beside her, clicked his boots from his skis with his poles and knelt to grip her shoulder. 'Are you hurt?'

The white world gradually steadied. 'Banged my head,' she said. 'But nothing's broken.'

He swore. 'Bloody fools, they were all over the place. Keep still. Where did you hurt your head?'

She put a hand to a tender, sore lump, and winced.

Zachary swore again. 'Let me see.' He bent over her, stripped off his gloves, and gently parted her hair. 'Mmm. That's a nasty bump. Are you feeling dizzy at all?'

'No, not really.'

'Not really?' He frowned and shifted his hands to either side of her face, lifting it so he could study her.

'I mean, it's gone now. I'm all right.' Except for the way her heart was hammering away.

Another skier slid to a stop nearby. 'You okay?'

'Yes,' she said.

'Hang on,' Zachary requested of the man. Turning to her, he said, 'We can get medicos up here if you might be concussed.'

'I'm sure I'm not, honestly.'

He studied her again, then nodded to the would-be Samaritan. 'We're okay, thanks.' The man gave them a wave and carried on downhill.

Katrien scooped up a handful of snow and pressed it to the bruise.

'You should wear a hat,' he said.

'I took it off in the café and forgot it.'

'Why didn't you say so?' He looked irritated. 'If I'd known you had one with you I'd have made sure you put it on.'

She'd been afraid he might change his mind about accompanying her if she held him up. 'I'm sorry,' she said. 'I've spoiled your run again.'

'Don't worry about it. I have another five days.'

Had he opted for the same cut-rate package that she had taken? 'I haven't seen you at the hotel.'

'I'm staying at a friend's private lodge.' He paused. 'Were you looking for me at the hotel?'

Katrien blinked at him. 'What do you mean?'

Zachary studied her face consideringly. 'Never mind. Do you think you can stand, with my help?'

'Yes.' She could probably manage without it, but she didn't fancy floundering round trying to get her balance if she was wrong. She manoeuvred herself into position, then stood up slowly while he steadied her. His hand remained on her waist and he was looking down at her with a slightly amused, knowing expression.

'Thank you,' she said tightly. 'I can manage now.'

He didn't move and she cast him a fierce glare. 'I know I seem to have made a habit of looking to be in need of rescuing when you're around, but it wasn't deliberate. And I certainly didn't come up the mountain with the intention of waylaying you.' She was appalled that he might have thought so. 'I don't find climbers that fascinating, and anyway, in case you'd forgotten, I'm engaged to be married.'

'I hadn't forgotten,' he said. 'Had you?'

Katrien drew a deep, furious breath. 'No!' She'd done nothing that could be construed that way, she assured herself.

She stiffened against his light hold and put a hand behind her to tug at his wrist, but that was a mistake, making her body curve towards his just as he bent his head and increased the pressure of his hand on her waist against her ineffectual resistance. And said softly, 'Could I make you...forget?'

His voice, his face were those of the man in her dreams, and for a second she imagined that this was another night fantasy. Tongue-tied, she was possessed of a great curiosity. The air around them seemed stilled, waiting.

But when his mouth was a hairsbreadth from hers, she jerked away, assailed by a sudden shaft of familiar fear. 'No!'

'Okay,' Zachary said easily, releasing her. He picked up the pole she'd lost and handed it courteously to her. 'Only that isn't the message I've been getting from you.'

She looked up from pushing her gloved hand through the loop on the ski pole to see him regarding her with quizzical enquiry. Flushing, she realised he was right. Somehow in her mind he'd got mixed up with the larger-than-life figure who had dominated her dream life since adolescence. It wasn't his fault that she'd been giving out confusing signals. She was confused herself.

'The thing is,' she said, 'you remind me of someone I...met a long time ago.'

'Not your fiancé?'

Katrien shook her head.

'Does he know about this...someone?'

'There's nothing to know.'

'Nothing?' He gave a short, breathy laugh.

Katrien looked at him angrily, and he said, 'I'd say your fiancé has a problem on his hands.'

'It's not a problem,' she said emphatically. 'You don't understand.' Not that there was any need for him to do so.

'Does What's-his-name understand?'

'Callum,' she said. 'He has nothing to worry about, and excuse me, but it's none of your business.'

'Maybe it isn't. But I tell you what—if I were engaged to you and saw you looking at another man the way you look at me, I'd be worried all right. I'd be doing something about it.'

'Like what?' she shot at him without thinking.

He looked thoughtful. 'You probably don't want to know.'

Violence? Her lip curled with scorn. 'Of course, you rugged mountain men are so physical!'

'Yeah,' he said, his eyes glinting. 'We are.' His hand reached over, so casually, and cupped her chin, turning her face towards him. And then he leaned down and kissed her thoroughly, his lips exploring hers, parting them, mastering her with a flair and panache that he hadn't learned on any mountain slopes.

Anchored by her skis, hampered by the ski poles looped to her hands, she could hardly move. Pure panic fought with the hot sweep of passion that sent the blood racing in her veins and made her lips pliant and shame-fully eager under his.

Someone swished by with a whoop of laughter and someone else whistled shrilly across the snow. Katrien made a protesting sound and tried to tear herself from Zachary's hold.

He lifted his head and looked down at her. 'If I were your Callum,' he said, 'I'd be *very* worried.'

She pulled herself away, keeping her balance with some difficulty, and trying to breathe normally. 'That was...'

'Wonderful?' he suggested as she hunted for words.

'Unfair!' she snapped. 'Contemptible.'

His lips pursed. 'I didn't think my technique was that bad.'

He was laughing at her. 'You had no right to kiss me!'

'I didn't notice you complaining.'

'I'm complaining now!'

Zachary laughed. 'After the fact.'

'I could hardly do it before—I didn't know what you intended.'

He gave her a level look. 'You had a fair idea,' he drawled. And added, 'You wanted to know, too.'

About to deny it, she hesitated, and then clamped her teeth together. She *had* wanted to know—to know what he would do in Callum's place, what it would be like to be kissed by him. She'd almost invited him to do it.

Mortified, she turned away from him. 'Thank you for stopping. I'll be fine on my own now.'

But he paced her all the way, then followed without comment as she made for the chairlift going down. 'Is your head aching?' he asked her.

'No. It's just a bump.'

'If you feel unwell—'

'I'm not unwell. But I think I'll stick to the easy run after this.'

A chair arrived and she stepped forward. 'If that satisfies you,' he taunted quietly, standing aside as she took her seat and the safety bar came down in front of her.

Katrien stared straight ahead, refusing to look at him, and the chair lifted her into the air and carried her away from him.

She was in the hotel lounge bar, having a brandy after dinner and chatting with two American girls, when she saw Zachary come in, dressed in cords and a chunky natural wool sweater. He looked around the room, found her and gave her a nod, then approached the bar.

Katrien forced her attention back to her companions, but was aware of Zachary getting his drink and then crossing the room to them.

When he stopped before their table she had to look up and acknowledge his presence.

'Hello, Katrien.' He pulled her woollen hat from a back pocket and dropped it on the table. 'I thought you might be missing this.'

'Thank you,' she said, staring at it.

'May I?' he asked politely, including the two Americans in his enquiring glance.

'Oh, sure!' One of them moved her chair over to make room for him to take the empty fourth at the table.

Katrien introduced him, and watched him charm the girls with his smile and stories of the mountains. But when she had finished her brandy and made to go he put down his glass and stood up. 'Nice meeting you,' he told the American girls, and followed Katrien from the room.

In the foyer he said, 'I hoped to talk to you.'

'What for?'

Taking her arm, he drew her over to where a couple of armchairs were placed at either side of a low table.

Reluctantly she sat down, and he took the other chair, leaning forward with his hands clasped between his knees. 'To apologise,' he said, 'for imagining you were deliberately putting yourself in my way. And for the kiss…though it's hard to say I'm sorry about that. I enjoyed it too much.'

He wasn't the only one, she thought guiltily. 'Thank you,' she said. 'Apology accepted. I guess…you couldn't be blamed for wondering if I was pursuing you. I suppose women do.'

His mouth twitched in a half smile. 'Not often enough. I was going to buy you a drink, but—'

They couldn't return to the bar now. 'I'll take a rain-check on that,' she offered.

'Right. I'll hold you to it.' He leaned back, smiling at her in a relaxed fashion. 'You're a model, aren't you? That'll be why I thought I recognised you at the dinner when…we met.'

Was that why he'd stared at her, as she'd stared at him? She was used to people knowing who she was, or not knowing but being aware they'd seen her face somewhere. And yet she'd thought there was something different, some special awareness about the way he'd kept looking at her. Maybe she had simply imagined it because of her own sense of recognition, her conviction that he was the man who haunted her sleep.

'You've probably seen some of my magazine work,' she suggested. 'Or maybe a TV ad.'

'I think I'd remember if I'd seen you on TV. I don't watch much, and the last few years I've been out of the country most of the time.'

'Climbing.'

'Yes. In India, South America…wherever there are

mountains.' Perhaps he saw something in her face. 'You don't approve?'

Katrien shrugged. 'I don't understand the compulsion. When you talked about it that night I could see you were in love with the mountains. But it seems so...'

'Pointless?' Zachary laughed. 'Only those who do it truly understand. It's a matter of pitting yourself against the elements, experiencing the worst that nature can throw at you, and coming out on top. Of proving yourself *to* yourself.'

'Over and over? Until you die? Like your friend Ben?'

His face went smooth and expressionless, and she said swiftly, 'I'm sorry. I didn't mean to remind you.'

Zachary shook his head. 'It's okay.' He was silent for a moment, gazing down at his brown leather boots. 'I'm used to losing my friends to the mountains. Not many of us live to a ripe old age.'

Inexplicably angry, she said, 'So it's acceptable? You can just shrug your shoulders and say, "Poor old Ben"—or poor old Dick or Tom or Harry?'

'It's not like that. But on the mountains you realise how little one human life really matters in the scale of things. And Ben died doing—'

'What he wanted to do. I know.' Her voice was decidedly tart. 'And he left a wife and family behind while he went off to do it.'

'Wendy knew what she was taking on when she married him. They used to climb together before the children came along.'

'And then she gave it up, but he didn't?'

Zachary spread his hands. 'Climbing was his life.'

'And yours?'

There was a moment's silence. 'I'm not married.'

He would be about thirty, Katrien guessed, a few

years older than herself. 'Have you ever been married?' she asked.

He was looking at her, his eyes dark. 'A couple of near-misses. They wanted me to give up climbing.' He gave her a crooked smile.

'I rest my case.' She stood up and he followed. 'I'll see you around, Mr Ballantine.'

She made to pass him on the way to the stairs, but he reached out and caught at her arm. 'Tomorrow?' he urged. 'On the top ski field? I wouldn't like to think you were staying away from the upper level because of me.'

There was no need for her to stay away. He'd apologised, they both understood the situation, and nothing more was likely to happen. What could happen on a popular ski slope with dozens of people about?

Temptation warred with common sense. She temporised, knowing it was weak and stupid. 'Maybe.'

CHAPTER THREE

WHEN Katrien arrived next day at the upper field Zachary was coming out of the café. As she saw him pick up his skis she told herself it was coincidence, that he hadn't been sitting and watching the chairlift, waiting for her.

He smiled at her lazily and, without speaking at all, tramped to her side at the top of the slope, let her push off before him, and followed, swooping past her in a series of sashaying curves, wide sweeps leaving parabolic lines in the snow.

She began to copy him, watching how he used his body, feeling her own muscles respond as she mimicked his movements.

She finished the run faultlessly and came to a swerving halt beside Zachary, flushed and proud of herself and meeting his eyes unafraid, responding to their laughing approval.

'I never thought I was that good!' she said involuntarily.

'We none of us know what we can do until we try.' He smiled at her, and suggested, 'I'll buy you a drink before we do it again.'

She let him, but the next time she bought the drinks and he just raised a dark eyebrow at her and allowed her to pay.

They skied together every day, and had coffee or drinks afterwards. One afternoon he asked her if it had always been her ambition to become a model, and she laughed and told him the only career she'd seriously considered was librarianship, which made him laugh in turn. 'I was in my last year at school,' she said, 'and a friend asked me to model a dress she'd designed for a sewing contest. We came third, and one of the judges approached me and asked if I was interested in modelling professionally. My friend was terribly excited and talked me into going to see the agency the woman suggested. And…well, things just sort of developed from there. What about you? How does one become a mountaineer?'

'I've been skiing since I was ten, more interested in cross-country than downhill. When I was fifteen I started climbing. At university I met Ben and we climbed together during the holidays.'

'What did you take at university?'

'A science degree.'

'Is that how you got a job in Antarctica?'

'Uh-huh. I studied ice movement, and did a fair bit of climbing there. Later Ben and I did Everest together, and then turned professional.'

'You make a living climbing mountains?'

'As mountain guides, nursemaiding recreational climbers to the best climbs around the world. In between, we tackled the real stuff, the places and routes no one had successfully climbed before.'

'Surely it's very expensive fitting out an expedition.'

'I've had grants from various institutions to carry out scientific studies on the mountains—the qualities of ice and snow, geological information, environmental studies. And several clothing and equipment firms helped finance our climbs. Ben was good at rustling up sponsors, and he was very photogenic.' Zachary grinned, half sadly. 'He even did a bit of modelling work. I teased him about that. You never bumped into him?'

Katrien shook her head. 'Your family must worry about you.'

'My mother was killed in a car accident when I was fourteen, and my father died a few years ago of a brain tumour. I have a brother who lives in England with his wife and family. We keep in touch, but his life is too busy to spend it worrying about me.'

'That was awfully young to lose your mother.' She still felt grief for her father's death over a year ago. How much worse it must have been for a fourteen-year-old.

'Death is the inevitable consequence of life.' He paused. 'I learned that a bit earlier than most people, I guess.'

Too early, surely. 'Is that why you took up climbing?' she asked, wondering if having his mother taken from him at a vulnerable age was what drove him to risk his life over and over—a need to defy the cruel fate that had taken her from him, to shake his fist in the face of death.

'It took my mind off things, certainly. When you're climbing you need to concentrate on your next step all the time. If you don't, it could be your last.'

'That's what I meant.'

He looked surprised, then searching. 'What you meant?'

She shouldn't have started this, but he was waiting for her to explain. 'I just thought…maybe you wanted to show that you could…beat death at his own game, because of your mother.'

Perhaps she had offended him. He seemed disconcerted. 'I suppose,' he said slowly, 'you could be right. I've never thought of it in those terms.'

She smiled apologetically. 'I didn't mean to psycho-analyse you.'

'That's okay.' He was staring at her as if seeing her

in an entirely new light. She looked down and fiddled with her coffee cup, until he pushed back his chair and said, 'Right, shall we go back to the run?'

On her fifth day when she arrived at the café he wasn't there. She unstrapped her skis and drank two cups of coffee she didn't want before she saw a figure in the distinctive ski suit riding up on the chairlift.

When she came to the door he smiled at her and said, 'I'm glad you waited.'

She didn't deny it. Of course she'd waited. The thought intruded that she'd waited a long time for him. Years.

Nonsense. He was just a man, met casually and probably never to be seen again. A very attractive man, but not the first one she'd found sexually appealing. She was bound to meet attractive men even after her marriage to Callum, and she would have to deal with that.

Her dreams had been empty lately; no dark, mysterious figure held her close and murmured in her ear, carried her against his heart.

She was too tired to dream. But it was the kind of healthful tiredness that left her looking forward to the next day and the white, beckoning snow. And each day her skiing had improved, her skills growing as she exerted herself, pushing herself to the limit of her ability in an effort to match Zachary.

The run was clear for once of other skiers, except near the bottom.

They took off side by side, and then Zachary swooped off to the left.

Katrien swerved right, glancing at Zachary to see when he changed direction, and in the same instant she followed, gliding back to meet him.

She saw him laugh, and knew he'd read her mind.

They passed in the middle of the run, missed each other narrowly and started new opposing curves.

With any other partner this would have been crazy— she wasn't nearly good enough to successfully negotiate the hairsbreadth manoeuvres—but she knew he would compensate for her, that she could trust him to get them safely down.

When they made it, to a spattering of applause from a group of people waiting to be transported to the top, she laughed up at him and they slapped gloved hands together in triumph.

She looked back up the slope at the almost perfect series of figure eights in the snow, some cut across by following skiers, and gasped. 'I don't believe we did that.'

As an experience it was unrepeatable. Almost superstitiously she knew that trying again would be an anticlimax.

As if he knew it too, Zachary said, 'Nothing beats the first time.'

Katrien supposed that was why he kept looking for more mountains to climb, peaks that hadn't been scaled before. She said, 'Tomorrow's my last day.'

He looked up the mountain, past the skiers zooming down the slopes, to the high, untouched snow beyond them. Then he looked back at her and said almost urgently, 'Come climbing with me.'

'Climbing?'

'You've never tried it, have you?'

Dumbly, Katrien shook her head.

'Nothing difficult. An easy, beginners' climb. Today I can teach you some of the basic techniques, and what to do in a fall so you don't just go on sliding out of control. We'll find a nice gentle slope to practise on. But we'll need to get you kitted up before starting an actual climb.'

'You'll be bored.'

A strange expression flitted across his face. He looked back up again at the mountain, his profile grim and shuttered. 'I promise you I won't be bored.'

He had some gear in the back of his four-wheel-drive, and he found an easy slope not far from the ski run and showed her how to hold an ice axe when climbing, and use it as a brake, as an aid to help herself up a slope, and to probe the snow and discover if it was really firm or just a crust on top of loose powder. He taught her techniques for controlling a fall, and how to work with a partner on a rope.

He asked for her boot size, and next morning called for her at the hotel when it was barely dawn, bringing climbing gear, including boots and crampons and a helmet for her. 'Borrowed them,' he told her briefly.

He made her go over what she'd learned, and demonstrated how to remove snow from the spikes of her crampons with an ice axe. 'You have to keep them free because if your crampons are balled up they can't grip the slope.'

They had something to eat first, then signed a book for the park rangers stating their intended route and estimated return time, and set out to climb the mountain.

He roped her to him, even though the first part was an easy walk over a gentle incline where their boots left deep indents in the snow. 'Don't let the rope go slack,' he reminded her.

When the going got steeper she was glad of the rope and of Zachary's tutelage. He led on the upward slopes but made her go ahead on the downward side of a ridge so if she got into trouble he could help her. She was panting and her temples and upper lip were dampened with sweat when he hauled her onto a rugged bluff and declared, 'Okay, we can rest here for a while.'

There was sweat on his forehead too, although he wasn't flushed with exertion like her. The cold air seemed to have bleached the outdoor tan from his cheeks. He wiped his face with a gloved hand, staring out at the surrounding countryside—bleak and brown near the mountain, mistily green further away.

Katrien subsided on the snow. 'And you do this for fun?'

He glanced down at her and laughed shortly. 'You're not enjoying it?'

She gazed about them and admitted, 'The view is pretty spectacular.'

'Worth it?'

But she wasn't ready to concede that. 'How far are we going?' She squinted at the forbidding wall of rock—in some places too steep to hold the snow—that loomed above them.

He didn't answer immediately, but stood up and she turned to look at him, shading her eyes because the sun lay behind him, making his features dark and indistinguishable. Her heart thumped once with a quick, irrational, complicated emotion, a stirring of familiarity.

'How far,' he asked her, 'do you want to go?'

'Not all the way,' she answered. Then quickly added, 'We couldn't make it to the summit in the time we've got, could we?'

'No,' he agreed, after a tiny pause. 'Not if you don't feel ready for it.'

When she began to get cold she pushed herself to her feet. 'All right, MacDuff,' she sighed. 'Let's move on.'

'You're game?' He glanced at the unwelcoming terrain above them.

'If you are,' she agreed lightly.

He gave her an oddly searching look, then a faint smile. 'Remember what I told you. Let me know if you're in trouble.'

It was all right at first, hard work but not difficult. Perhaps she became too cocky, but as she went ahead of him across a virgin slope the snow suddenly seemed to disappear under her boots and she shrieked Zachary's name, desperately trying to remember and follow his earlier instructions.

She slid over a hidden overhang and found herself dangling in space, witless with terror. But Zachary had stopped the fall, and when her vision cleared she could see him leaning backwards further up the slope, his boots firmly dug into the snow.

She followed his calm, succinct directions, and with his help was able to crawl back onto the snow-covered slope. He held the rope firm, reefing it in as she panted towards him.

She collapsed into his arms, her breath coming in shuddering gasps. 'An easy beginners' climb, you said!'

'You're okay.' His breath feathered her ear as his arms tightened round her. 'It's all right, I won't let you go.'

She shivered, echoes of dreams reverberating in her mind, shards of memory kaleidoscoping and, rearranging themselves into a well-known pattern.

'You…saved my life,' she said, her voice sounding odd in her own ears.

His arms loosened and he gripped her shoulders. 'Nothing so dramatic. But,' he added, frowning, 'I should have known better than to drag you up here with me.'

'Drag me…?' She hadn't needed any coercion; she could scarcely claim he'd forced her. Then, looking down at the nylon line that still joined them, she made a little grimace. 'Well, you could say that, I suppose...'

She raised her eyes to his, willing him to laugh, and after a moment he did, in a slightly strained way, releasing his hold on her. 'You're a brave woman.'

Brave? Katrien shook her head. 'Hardly.' But now wasn't the time to detail her fears and phobias. And Zachary Ballantine, mountaineer, wasn't a person who would understand them. 'Did you ever,' she asked him carefully, her heart thudding, 'save someone's life?'

His eyes went dark, his mouth straight. 'I didn't save Ben's.'

She felt again the wave of pain that had emanated from him the night of the charity dinner when he'd spoken of his friend. Stretching out her gloved hand, she grasped one of his. None of the usual platitudes would suffice, she knew. He'd probably heard them all dozens of times.

He didn't look up, but his hand closed hard about hers through the layers of insulating fabric. He lifted their clasped hands and brought them down once, on his knee.

They sat in silence for a few minutes, then by tacit consent got up and continued the traverse. At the next vantage point Zachary said, 'Time to start going down.'

Katrien was surprised at her sense of disappointment, but there had never been any question that they would attempt to make the summit. She followed him obediently, and heeded his warning not to relax just because they were no longer climbing. 'More lives are lost on the descent,' he said, 'when people get careless.'

A light snowfall had started before they signed in again at the foot of the mountain. When they emerged from the building dusk was falling and the snowflakes drifting across the car park had thickened, driving against the building.

They paused in the porch and Zachary said, 'I'll drop you off at the hotel.'

Katrien shivered, hugging herself. 'That would be very welcome, thank you.' She didn't feel like waiting about for public transport.

'Wait here.' He strode off into the flurrying snow.

A few minutes later a four-wheel-drive vehicle drew up before the porch, and Zachary dropped to the ground and opened the other door for her. 'Hop in.'

He had turned on the heater, and blessedly warm air curled about her feet when he restarted the motor. All the way to the hotel she formulated and discarded things to say. Zachary drove with his eyes on the road ahead, obscured by the whirling snow that platted continuously against the windscreen. The wind was increasing by the minute. She thought he'd been wise to get them down from the mountain not only before dark but before the snowstorm had begun. Surely it hadn't been forecast.

He drew up close to the hotel's main doorway.

'Thank you,' she said. How inadequate and thin it sounded, 'And thank you for taking me on the mountain.'

'I wanted you with me.' With a curious air of hesitation, he looked away for a moment. 'Have dinner with me.'

She glanced at the lighted doorway of the hotel. 'Where?'

Zachary considered the question. 'Would you come back to the lodge?'

'Who else is there?'

He paused again before answering. 'My friends are overseas. There's just me.' He was half turned to face her, his forearm resting on the steering wheel while he waited for Katrien's decision.

'With this snow,' she said slowly, 'we might be stranded there.'

'Yes,' Zachary agreed gravely. 'We might.' Another pause. 'Would you object?'

She had difficulty getting the words to leave her lips. 'Callum might.' Reminding both of them.

Zachary nodded. 'Uh-huh.'

She couldn't do that to Callum. Or to herself. The strange pull this man exerted on her senses, her subconscious, didn't justify her cheating on her fiancé, betraying her own principles and jeopardising her entire future. 'I can't.'

He nodded again, as though her answer was the one he'd expected. 'I guess not.' He shifted in his seat, his chest lifting on a breath. 'How about here, then? In the dining room. Your fiancé couldn't take exception to that, could he?'

Gratefully she seized on the reprieve. 'I'm sure he wouldn't. That would be...nice.'

It would be a lifeline. Callum would certainly have every reason to object if he knew that the stark necessity of saying goodbye to Zachary Ballantine was stifling her breath and freezing her blood. That the prospect of never seeing him again sent her into an irrational, mindless panic.

'I'll go back to the lodge and freshen up,' Zachary was saying. 'See you about seven?'

She nodded. Too late to back out now, she told herself with guilty relief. 'Drive carefully. No, don't get out, I can manage.' She was scared to be touched by him again. She didn't know how she was going to get through a meal with him without him guessing at what she felt. But at least she'd had the sense to insist on a public place.

As soon as she got into her room she tried to phone

Callum. She needed to talk to him, hear his voice, remind herself that the man she was going to marry was waiting for her in Auckland. Remind herself why she loved him—his innate kindness and sensitivity, his humour, his rock-solid integrity. If Callum had taken a week off without her she was certain beyond doubt that he wouldn't have spent it with another woman.

The phone rang, and then Callum's answering machine cut in. She put down the receiver, considered, then rang again and left a carefully worded message. 'I'm having dinner with someone here in the dining room. It's snowing. See you tomorrow night. I love you.'

Why did that feel so traitorous?

She ought to call Zachary. *Sorry, dinner's off. Thanks and goodbye.*

She didn't know where to contact him.

Leave a message for him at the desk. Say you can't make it after all.

And have dinner in her room? Skulking there like a coward? She ought at least to have the decency to say it to his face.

Say what? I made a mistake. I shouldn't have agreed to have dinner with you. I've changed my mind.

Why?

Why? Because I'm afraid. Afraid of the effect you have on me. Afraid of how tempted I was to spend the night at your friends' lodge with you. Afraid of my own weakness. Afraid because you are the personification of my dreams...those dreams that are both erotic and terrifying.

Afraid of finding out that you are who I think you are...or that you're not.

She showered and changed into a fine wool skirt and soft mohair sweater. Touched her eyelashes with mascara and used a smidgen of shadow on the lids, but left her mouth unpainted.

When she came down to the lobby Zachary was waiting for her. His casual trousers, boots and V-necked fisherman's rib over a jade-green shirt did nothing to diminish his confident masculinity.

He didn't smile as she walked towards him. But he took his hands from the pockets of the trousers and held one out to her. She put hers into it without a thought, and stood looking at him.

'Want a drink first?' he asked her.

Maybe she needed just one. 'I'll have a Vault 88.'

He steered her to the lounge bar, found a banquette for them, and went to get the drinks.

Katrien sipped hers slowly. A man across the room was staring at her. He nudged the woman at his side and she stared too. Katrien looked away and regarded the liquid remaining in her glass.

'Are you regretting this?' Zachary's voice made her lift her head.

'Why should I?' she countered, wondering if he could read her uncertainty so easily.

'You seem…distracted.'

'I tried to phone Callum,' she told him. 'He wasn't home.'

'To ask his permission?'

'I don't need his permission. Our relationship isn't like that.'

'What is it like?' He leaned towards her as though really wanting an answer.

Katrien gave him a guarded look and he shrugged. 'Out of order,' he conceded. 'I withdraw the question.' He picked up the beer he'd ordered and drank some. 'So…you're not worried that maybe he's out with some other woman?'

'I know he's not.'

'Supposing he was—would it bother you?'

'If he was it would be perfectly innocent. I know I can trust him.'

'As he trusts you?'

Katrien turned her glass. 'Yes. As he has every reason to trust me.'

But she couldn't look at him as she said it.

'Okay,' he said after a moment. 'I get the message, Katrien.'

Katrien lifted her glass to distract him from the flush on her cheeks, and finished her drink. Had she been so crudely obvious?

'So...' he drained his glass and glanced at her empty one '...shall we have dinner? Or would you like another drink?'

'I don't want any more.' She slid out of the banquette. 'And mountain climbing makes me hungry.'

The food was delicious, and the wine Zachary ordered helped her to relax. He didn't drink much of it, and she remembered he had to drive the utility vehicle back to the lodge on the snow-covered road. 'You've got chains on the ute, haven't you?'

'Sure. I always have them.'

They kept the conversation on a superficial plane, talking about current affairs, the latest Oscar-winning film, a little about countries they'd both visited. He had seen the wild places—the Rockies, the Andes, the Southern Alps. She knew the cities—Melbourne and Sydney, London, New York. 'But even when I'm on an assignment,' she told him, 'I try to see things outside the centres.'

He mentioned a climbing trip in Wales, and she said, 'When I was in England I went to Hay-on-Wye, on the Welsh border. Have you been there?'

'Does it have mountains?'

Katrien laughed. 'Mountains of books. It's a tiny town packed with bookshops. I spent a day there and came away with a suitcase full of books, most of them second-hand.'

'You're obviously fond of reading.'

'There's a lot of waiting time in modelling. It can get very boring while they're setting up a shoot and the art director and the photographer argue about how it should go. I'd go mad if I didn't have something to do, and reading is one of my great pleasures.'

'I know what you mean. I've spent days dug into a snow cave in a blizzard. One time in the Antarctic, by the time the wind died I could have repeated the whole of *Moby Dick* backwards.'

That set them off discovering mutual favourites and swapping recommendations.

'Travel books,' Katrien said. 'I love them.'

'Why read about it when you can do it?'

'Some people can't do it, so they like to read about it. You've never written about your adventures?'

'Some climbers write for *National Geographic* or travel magazines. At that dinner a publisher approached me about doing a book telling the story of the expedition. I told him I'd think about it so long as the proceeds could go to the fund for Wendy and the kids.' Zachary shrugged. 'But I'm no writer.'

I am, it was on the tip of her tongue to tell him. Under the name of Kate Winston she'd written travel articles for magazines, sometimes the same ones in which she appeared in fashion features or advertisements.

Their coffee came, and she realised that the evening was almost over. The time had passed too swiftly.

Trying to formulate the question that had been hovering at the edge of her mind ever since the night she'd laid eyes on Zachary Ballantine, she watched the steam rise from the cup between her hands. Where should she start? If she asked him straight out of the blue would he think she was crazy?

Surely after this week he knew she wasn't. She took a deep, unsteady breath and raised her eyes. And saw him looking at her with an intensity that stopped her heart.

Her eyes widened, her own breath trapped in her chest. 'What is it?' she whispered.

'Do you have any idea,' he said, his voice husky and slow, 'how blindingly lovely you are?' As if the words had broken some spell, he leaned back a little, and his mouth took on a wry, self-mocking curve. 'Stupid question. Of course you do. You probably get told so a dozen times a day.'

'Not necessarily.' Some photographers had a patter of meaningless compliments and pet names—'Come on, angel, sweet-face, give me a pout now. Yeah, baby, let me have it with your eyes, okay? Great, a bit more skin, huh? Hold it there, gorgeous—' Others were as likely to snarl, 'God, are you a woman or a stick insect? Can't you at least try to look interested? That hair—I said *casual*, not bloody bird's nest.'

'Do you enjoy your job?' he asked curiously. 'When you're not waiting around?'

'I like the variety, the talented people I meet, the travel, and it can be exciting when we're meeting a deadline or we have a really good photographer and an art director with original ideas. Although they're sometimes very uncomfortable ideas. One had us shooting in the Australian desert on camels, wearing evening gowns! Camels are the most bad-tempered creatures on earth. They dribble and spit, and they're more stubborn than donkeys.'

'Not the high point of your career, I take it.'

'Oh, it was, if you like to take that literally. I was supposed to perch on one beast's back and look glamorous in a chiffon gown while I rode it round in circles. They told me if I could ride a horse I could manage a camel, but they forgot to tell the camel. The brute took off—not terribly fast, but from where I was sitting up on that hump the ground was a long way down. I know why they're called ships of the desert. You get seasick on them.'

He laughed. 'It sounds less than fun. If you get seasick on land, how do you get on if you're asked to pose on board a boat?'

'I keep away from them,' she said curtly, dropping her gaze. 'I hate the sea.'

'Hate it? And you a New Zealander!'

'Yes, well...' This was her chance. 'There's a reason for that.'

The teasing light died from his eyes as he scanned her face. 'Do you want to tell me about it?'

Katrien moistened her lips. 'Something happened when I was just fourteen. Before that I was quite happy on the sea—or in it. Our family used to spend every summer at the beach.'

'Mine too. A great New Zealand tradition.'

Katrien smiled thinly. 'My father loved to get away from the city and fish from his dinghy. Mum just sunbathed and read books while my sister and I were in the water, swimming and surfing.'

That summer had been like any other, except that she and Miranda had discovered boys. Or boys had discovered them. Miranda, eleven months older than Katrien, at nearly fifteen had a well-developed figure. Katrien had been a late developer. Taller than her older sister and built on coltish lines, she had finally acquired a neat and nicely rounded bust. But while Miranda was covertly fascinated by the teenage males who paraded about the beach with their surfboards, noisily shoving and pushing each other, Katrien was largely unimpressed by their showing off their prowess in the waves, and even less captivated by their clumsy attempts to pick up her and her sister. Mostly her sister, she'd noted with more relief than envy.

Miranda was willing to entertain the advances of a few would-be beach Lotharios, while their mother watched from a discreet and amused distance. Katrien was still more interested in the heroes who populated the paperback romances and hardback classics in her bedside bookcase, and the poster of Michelangelo's *David* pinned to the wall of her bedroom. While Miranda chatted to this boy or that, Katrien tried to gauge whether her sister wanted a chaperon, or someone to divert the attention of the current favourite's less good-looking friend, or whether the situation called for a younger sister to remove herself and go for a swim.

Having chosen the latter course one day, hoping she'd correctly read the signals, she had swum out beyond the breakers and was floating lazily on the calmer water. A big swell lifted her, and she changed her position, paddling along a little on the other side of it.

There was a surfboarder nearby, waiting for a wave, his back to her as he knelt on the board. He wore sleek, tight swim-briefs and when he stood up, poised himself on the gently swaying board ready for the next incoming swell, he resembled a work of art. Watching, she experienced the same stirring of admiration and pleasurable, all-over warmth that she felt when she studied Michelangelo's sculpture.

She watched him ride in, catching the wave and perfectly balanced on its crest, then curving down into it as it broke, board and man disappearing from her sight.

She swam further out, and then turned to make her way in to the beach. She was an experienced swimmer and had often been this far before. At first she didn't realise why it was taking so long for the shore to seem closer. Then she felt the tug of the current and her heart lurched with fear. She'd swum into a rip.

Don't panic, she exhorted herself. Don't fight the current. Swim across it. In theory she knew what to do. It was just harder than she'd ever imagined.

The lifeguards would see her if she floated on her back and raised an arm, but Katrien shrank from making a fuss. Surely she must be able to find the edge of the rip, get back to safe water? Only she felt herself being pulled further out to sea despite her efforts, and she was getting tired.

There was some sort of commotion closer to the shore. She could see a flurry of action, several people in an inflatable boat. The lifeguards were in the water.

They were coming for her. She stopped swimming with sheer relief, and found herself gulping seawater, sinking. Surfacing hurriedly, she floated, tiredly moving her arms. She should swim towards the lifeguards, make it easier for everyone.

There were a lot of people further in towards the shore. A lot of activity. With disbelief she watched them all retreat to the beach, and realised what had happened.

The rip must have appeared suddenly, and she wasn't the only one caught in it. The lifeguards had their hands full, busy rescuing other people. Katrien hadn't waved, hadn't attracted anyone's attention. No one had noticed her. She felt cold, afraid.

Truly frightened now, she tried to shout to them, and swallowed more salty water. Coughing, she turned onto her back ready to raise an arm in a signal for help, but was convulsed with another cough and found herself going under again.

I'm a good swimmer, she told herself. I won't drown. I can't!

She kicked out with her legs and a shaft of pain seized the muscles without any warning at all. Her mouth opened in an involuntary effort at a scream before the water filled it and dragged her down.

She tried to hold her breath, but in the strange, eerie underwater stillness everything seemed to be going black, and there was no sound but the bubbling roar in her ears. I'm going to die, she thought, astonished rather than frightened. Her chest hurt, and her legs wouldn't move, and the roar in her ears became louder. And then she must have lost consciousness.

CHAPTER FOUR

'WHAT happened?' Zachary's quiet voice asked.

She realised she'd been sitting mute, reliving the nightmare with her hands clenched on her coffee cup, the contents cooling.

Carefully she put down the cup. 'I nearly drowned,' she said, 'caught in a rip. I could maybe have coped with the rip, because I was quite a strong swimmer. But then I got cramp. So badly I couldn't help myself at all. I thought I was going to die.'

'But you didn't.'

Katrien shook her head. 'There was a surfboarder. He saw I was in trouble and came to the rescue, pulled me out of the water and hauled me up onto his board. Gave me mouth-to-mouth and took me in to the shore. I was very lucky.'

'I guess you were.' He was staring at her. She stared back, unblinking, trying to recall every detail of that day years ago.

By the time the surfboarder had got her back to the beach her mother and Miranda had become alarmed and told the lifeguards she was still out there. Two of the guards were on their way into the water when Katrien and her rescuer made it through the breakers.

They'd tried to take over from him, but Katrien wouldn't let them. Scared and disoriented, she'd clung to the man who had saved her, and in the end he'd left the board for the lifeguards to bring in for him, and swung her into his arms to carry her through the shallows. Sobbing, she had hung onto him, her arms locked about his neck, her eyes blurred by tears of shock, until she'd heard her mother's anxious voice and felt herself lowered to the sand. Not until then had she let go her hold on him.

With her mother's arms about her, she had looked up and seen him standing there with the sun behind him, his face just a dark shadow as she squinted against the dazzle and the tears that still filled her eyes.

She'd ducked her head to wipe away the tears, and when she looked up again he'd disappeared. Miranda was there, crying in sympathy and fright, hugging her, people had been milling about staring or offering advice, and one of the lifeguards brought an oxygen mask over and said they should get her to hospital for a medical check. She'd tried to ask 'Where is he?' but her voice was scarcely audible and she started to cough, her throat raw and salt-abraded. And nobody heard.

Someone had called an ambulance and they'd put her in hospital overnight for observation. By the time anyone else thought to look for the surfboarder he was gone.

Her father had talked to a news reporter, and run an ad in the personal column, because he'd wanted to thank the man who had rescued his daughter. But no one had come forward.

'I never had a chance to thank him,' she told Zachary. 'He brought me in and then walked away. I never even knew who he was.'

'Does it matter?'

'I think if someone saves your life you owe them at least a decent thank-you. Don't you?'

'Maybe he didn't want to be thanked.'

'Why not?'

Zachary shoved away his coffee cup, then lifted a finger and ran it round the rim, his eyes leaving hers. 'When you're climbing,' he said, 'you have to depend on your partner, or your team. I've lost count of the times I've "saved" someone, or they've saved me. It's part of the business.'

'So it's no big deal to you?'

He shrugged.

Katrien stared at him steadily. 'When I said today that you'd saved my life, I didn't mean just then. I meant years ago, when I was a teenager.' He seemed to wince slightly, but she went on stubbornly, 'It was you in the surf that day. And now at last I have the opportunity to tell you how grateful I am.'

Almost impatiently, Zachary shook his head. 'Katrien, I don't want to hear this.'

'But I want to say it. After all this time, I need to say all the things I didn't—'

'Why now?' he interrupted. 'Why wait until tonight? You had the chance at that dinner, and all this week.'

Because she'd been afraid her mind was playing tricks on her, that she'd simply experienced a random attraction to a total stranger, and her subconscious had superimposed his face on her dream lover, made him the embodiment of her secret fantasy. And because she'd been afraid of making a fool of herself if she was wrong. 'I wasn't absolutely sure it was you. Not until today on the mountain.'

'What difference did that make?'

How could she explain it? 'I just knew, when you...' When you held me in your arms and calmed me with your touch, your voice. That familiar voice, that touch that I have always known.

'When you fell.' He sounded rather scornful.

Katrien bit her lip. 'Yes. When you rescued me again. It came back to me then.'

He looked at her frowningly, and then with dawning enlightenment. 'You don't actually remember, do you?

You have no idea what your surfboarder looked like. If you did you'd have known right away if it was me, the first time you saw me.'

'I did know…sort of. I just found it hard to believe I'd…found you.'

'You did nothing about it.'

'There were so many people and…'

'And you weren't sure,' he insisted, his voice harsh.

'Are you angry because I wasn't?'

'I'm not angry.' He pushed a hand over his hair. 'I wasn't expecting this.'

Katrien smiled tentatively. 'I'm sorry if it embarrasses you. But I wanted you to know how grateful—'

'Yeah, all right. You told me.' He pulled his empty cup towards him again. 'I need more coffee. How about you?' He signalled to the waiter. When the man had gone again, he sat back in his chair and stared at Katrien. His eyes became glazed, as though he was recalling something from long ago. He shook his head and a fleeting, rueful smile appeared on his mouth.

'It *was* you, wasn't it?' She leaned forward eagerly. 'You pulled me out of the water.'

His eyes kindled into life, and an oddly cynical smile touched his mouth. 'Maybe that depends on just how grateful you are.'

Katrien flushed, her eyes widening, and he recanted immediately. 'No, forget I said that. Bad taste.'

Stupidly, for a moment she was almost disappointed. He'd been teasing, making a joke of it because he was uncomfortable with the role of hero.

Their coffee came, giving them a breathing space. The waiter presented a small folder, and Katrien said, 'I'll sign it to my room.'

'No, you won't.' Zachary took the folder from the

man and glanced inside before putting it down on the cloth. 'I invited you.'

'You could at least let me buy you a dinner, considering what you did for me.'

Zachary turned his coffee cup with his fingers, staring down at it. 'But how much do you really remember?' he asked her.

Her voice dropped to almost a whisper. 'I have dreams...'

He looked up. 'Nightmares?'

Katrien hesitated. 'Sometimes.'

'And you keep away from the sea. Have you had any counselling?'

Katrien nodded. She'd seen a counsellor for several months, after her family realised that her terror of the sea wasn't going to abate with time. Perhaps it might have helped more if she'd ever told about the dreams. But she'd never brought herself to speak to anyone about them. 'It's not a major problem,' she said. 'I just don't swim any more.' Which was why she refused to model swimsuits. The first time she'd agreed to do so, imagining that the shoot would take place in a studio, she'd been taken instead to a beach and told to stand in the rolling breakers and look as though she was enjoying herself.

She had flatly refused, and when they had insisted, created a scene verging on hysteria. In the end they'd settled for photographing her on the sand with the sea as a background, but she'd been jittery and stiff the whole time. The art director was disgruntled and the photographer had called her a temperamental bitch and said he'd never use her again. Her agent hadn't been pleased either, and when she'd informed him she wasn't ever going to do swimsuit work again he'd washed his hands of her.

It had been a setback to her career, but she'd gone to London and tried her luck there. Rather than explain her phobia, she simply told the agencies she applied to that she didn't do swimwear, and after several had laughed or sneered and brusquely dismissed her, one had taken her on despite the veto. Over the next few years she'd made a modest name for herself on the international circuit.

Then her father had become ill with the cancer that had slowly killed him, and she'd come home to New Zealand to be with him and help her mother and Miranda nurse him.

'You don't swim at all?' Zachary asked her now. 'Not even in a pool?'

She looked up at him again. 'Nobody ever died from *not* swimming.'

A faint smile curved his mouth. 'That's true.'

Katrien lifted her cup. 'I know it's trite,' she said, 'but I owe you my life. If I can ever help you...'

'You have,' he said, 'more than you know.'

'I...have?' Surprised, she stared at him over her poised cup.

He was apparently following the progress of one of the waiters across the room. When his eyes returned to her they were dark and brooding. 'All this week you've been there. And today...you trusted me to look after you on the mountain. You have no idea how much that means to me...right now.'

He was still grieving for the friend he hadn't been able to save, blaming himself for some kind of failure. So perhaps her willingness to follow him and believe that he'd keep her safe had been of some value.

'I knew you'd look after me,' she said.

'Will Callum?' he asked.

Startled at the change of subject, she blinked and hesitated. 'Yes,' she said with conviction. 'He's a kind, caring person. And he loves me.'

For a moment his mouth tightened. Then he said tonelessly, 'That's good. I wish you every happiness.'

He finished his coffee and pushed back his chair. 'I'd better start moving before I get snowed in.' He shoved several notes into the folder in which the waiter had presented the bill, and stood up.

Katrien got up too. 'Thank you for dinner—and everything else.' Thank you for my life.

He gave her a crooked little smile. 'My pleasure.'

'I'll come to the door with you.'

There were few people in the big lobby. It was much cooler than the dining room. Katrien followed Zachary to the outer doors, closed against the snow. 'Are you sure you'll be all right driving? How far away is the lodge?'

'Not far,' he reassured her. 'And I've driven in bad weather before.' He turned at the door and put a hand on her shoulder. 'Have a nice life with your Callum.'

She would, she was sure of it—wasn't she? 'Be careful on your mountains,' she replied huskily. Don't die young like Ben Storey and your other friends.

At the thought, she found herself putting out a hand to clutch at his woollen jersey. 'Please,' she whispered.

Maybe he misunderstood. Or maybe he didn't. His hand moved from her shoulder to slide up her nape, long fingers raking into her hair, tipping her head. Something disturbingly like anger flared in his eyes, and then his mouth descended on hers and her lips parted in response.

There was anger in his kiss, yes. And passion, and a desperate sorrow, so that she put her arms around him as much in a blind attempt at comfort as from the desire that flooded her body and made it tremble.

Then he put his hands on her shoulders and pushed

her away. Peripherally she was aware of movement in the lobby, of other people in the background, but none of that mattered, only the fierce green flame of Zachary's eyes.

His voice rasped, his breathing as uneven as hers. 'Was that gratitude?'

She swallowed. 'I just... It was goodnight,' she said shakily. 'Goodbye.'

He gave a short, harsh laugh. 'You sure give one hell of a goodnight kiss, lady.' He turned to the door and wrenched it open. Cold air rushed in and chilled her instantly to the bone. He looked back for a moment, and the snow outside whirled and flurried behind him. 'Goodbye, Katrien,' he said. And then he was gone, the door banging to behind him.

She lay awake for most of the night, trying to focus her thoughts on the coming reunion with her fiancé and dismally failing. Instead she found her consciousness filled with a dark face and deep green eyes, her mind returning over and over to the kiss in the cold outer lobby.

She got up early and packed, then ventured outside, well wrapped, to find a white world of snow. The vehicles in the car park had to be dug out, and the bus that took her to Taupo for her plane trip to Auckland drove through the blizzard that was blowing down the mountain. The temperature had dropped overnight to a record low.

Callum had left a loving message on her answering machine, and a promise to call that evening.

Katrien unpacked her bag and washed, dried and ironed. She cleaned the stove and the fridge, throwing out some fruit and cheese that had spoiled while she was away. She never kept much food in at any time, preferring to buy fresh ingredients when she planned to cook, but she'd got milk and half a dozen eggs on the way home.

She made French toast with sliced bread from her freezer compartment, reminding herself to get another loaf as there were only three slices left, and heated a can of soup. After washing up she showered and pulled on a jersey over warm track pants. When Callum arrived, bearing a bunch of daffodils and freesias, she thanked him extravagantly and said, 'I'll find a vase for them.'

He caught her as she turned away. 'Wait a minute.' He was smiling, drawing her into his arms, and she forced herself to smile back and return the lengthy, passionate kiss.

When the pressure of his mouth eased she drew away. 'We'll squash your lovely flowers.'

He let her go. 'Okay, shove them in some water and hurry back. Do you mind if I watch the rugby match for a while on TV? The All Blacks—'

'Go ahead, turn it on.' Sometimes she slightly resented his interest in the game. She liked to watch a well-played match herself, but with Callum it was almost a religion.

She got a vase and arranged the flowers, placing them in a corner on a brass side table she'd bought in Singapore. The flat had been a cream shell with a pale fawn carpet when she bought it, but the coloured rugs and quirky furniture she'd collected on her travels gave it life and personality.

Without taking his eyes from the screen, Callum held out a hand to her, and she went to join him on the sofa.

He put an arm about her shoulders and turned to nuzzle her neck, then straightened as a roar came from the television. 'Nearly missed it! What a try!'

Callum tucked her more snugly under his arm, and when the commercial break came on he turned to her again and gave her a lingering kiss. But as soon as the game recommenced his gaze returned to the screen.

'How was your trip?' he asked her idly during a dull patch, still watching.

'Fine. The weather was good. I improved my skiing a lot.'

'Good, that's good—hey, he can't do that! The ball was offside! What's wrong with this ref?'

Five minutes later he turned to Katrien again. 'No more flu?'

'Gone.'

'I'm glad.' He kissed her again and put both arms about her, pulling her half across his lap. 'I missed you.'

'I missed you too,' she replied dutifully.

He was bending his head when a cheer from the crowd on the TV made him lift it again.

'Sorry,' he said when the try had been safely converted. 'Where were we?'

Katrien held him off, laughing. 'You watch your game,' she said, sliding from his hold. 'I'll go and make us a pancake supper.'

His eyes lit up. He loved her pancakes. 'You are the most understanding woman in the world.'

Katrien smiled at him affectionately and went off to the kitchen. She had always appreciated Callum's down-to-earth ability to treat her like an ordinary woman, not some kind of goddess. Other men had tried to impress her with fancy restaurants and expensive shows. He preferred a quiet evening in her flat, or his inner-city apartment, and he liked her to cook for him, something she actually enjoyed.

In time she would forget this past week, she promised herself as she took eggs and milk from the refrigerator. And forget Zachary Ballantine, except as a man she had once spent some enjoyable but unimportant time with—

and to whom she owed an old, unrepayable debt of gratitude.

Now that she knew who he was and had expressed,
however inadequately, her thanks for that act of self-
lessness, surely she ought to be able to get on with her
life, freed from the haunting dreams.

She broke the eggs and began efficiently whisking
them. Another roar came from the living room, and
Callum cheered.

She smiled. Soon life would be back to normal.

Twenty minutes later she presented Callum with a
plate of pancakes drizzled with golden syrup. A news
preview was on: '...accuses the government of selling
taxpayers down the river,' the announcer was saying.
Katrien was still standing, her own plate in one hand, a
fork poised in the other, when the woman went on, 'And
a mountaineer who survived the ill-fated New Zealand
expedition in the Himalayas earlier this year has another
brush with death closer to home. Join us at nine-thirty
for the details.'

Katrien froze, her eyes going to the screen, where now
thirty men in shorts were running about on a muddy
field.

A brush with death? A mountaineer—Zachary? *Was
he hurt?*

'Sit down, darling,' Callum said, his mouth full of
pancake. 'This is delicious.'

'Callum?'

'Mmm?'

'Have they mentioned that before? The mountaineer?
Did they say who it was?'

He shook his head. 'Don't think so.' Looking up at
her, he swallowed a mouthful and frowned. 'What's the
matter?' He drew her down beside him. 'I didn't think
you knew any mountaineers.'

'I know Zachary Ballantine.'

'Well, we've spoken to him once. That doesn't make us friends, does it? I mean, I'd be sorry to hear that he's been injured or something, but—'

'No, *I* know him. I met him at the ski field. Met him again.'

'You didn't say.' He looked puzzled.

'I haven't had a chance to say,' she said defensively. 'You're more interested in the game!'

His face showed instant concern. 'Darling, I'm sorry! I didn't think you minded.' He found the remote control at his side and pressed the off switch.

'No, don't!' she protested. 'I want to watch it—the news.'

'Yes, of course.' He switched it on again, but turned down the sound. Then he placed his plate carefully on the floor and took hers too before reaching for her hands. 'So, what's it all about?' he asked gently.

'He was at Ruapehu,' she said. 'He...we recognised each other from the dinner. Remember, he thought I was going to faint that night and he—'

'Yes, of course I remember. And he wasn't likely to forget you. Did he make a play for you?'

'No!' she said hastily. 'Not really. He...he knew I was engaged.'

'I hope you told him I'd punch his nose in if he laid a finger on you.'

Callum was smiling and she tried to smile back. 'I told him I love you.' Had she? She couldn't recall actually saying the words. But Zachary had said he'd got the message. The message that she was loyal to her engagement.

Callum's eyes softened, and he leaned over and gently kissed her mouth. 'Thank you, darling.'

'I wanted to try skiing from the top field, and he offered to see me down because I hadn't done it before and I was a bit nervous.'

'A real gentleman.'

'He was being kind.'

'Uh-huh.'

'We spent some time together—on the slopes. And last night we had dinner at the hotel.'

'Katie—' Callum looked grave now '—why is this sounding like a confession?'

Her cheeks heated but she met his eyes squarely. 'It isn't a confession. It's an explanation.' But she had kissed Zachary goodnight—passionately.

Telling Callum that would only hurt him, and what good would it do? As for the other thing—

'Okay,' he said. 'Is that all you have to tell me?'

He knew her too well. 'I'd met him before,' she said, her eyes steady, willing him to understand. 'Before the night of the charity dinner.'

'You never mentioned it.' He frowned, puzzled.

'No, I...I wasn't sure then that it was him.'

'What are you talking about?'

She took a deep breath. 'I told you why I don't swim, remember?'

'Of course I remember.' Several times he'd suggested going to the Parakai hot pools near Auckland or to a beach, and after fobbing him off with vague excuses, eventually she'd had to confess to him that she didn't swim. His eager offer to teach her had forced her to explain her panicked refusal. 'You had a bad experience,' he acknowledged, 'and it scared you. I still think that if we took it slowly we could get you over it, you know. One day—'

'Yes, I know,' Katrien interrupted. They—or rather he—had discussed it more than once. But he would never force her. 'I told you someone saved me from drowning. That's who it was. Zachary Ballantine.'

He stared. 'It was?'

'Yes, he—' Katrien broke off as the news began. 'Turn it up.'

He still held one of her hands as they watched. The lead story was a political row, then there was an interview with the All Blacks' captain, and something about a warehouse fire. It seemed an eternity before the announcer mentioned the item they waited for. 'And a mountaineer who survived a Himalayan expedition in which one of his companions died and he himself suffered severe frostbite is in a serious condition in hospital. Zachary Ballantine's four-wheel-drive vehicle left a snow-covered road and rolled into a shallow, icy stream sometime between last night and—'

'No!' Katrien's hand went to her mouth.

'—midday today. Heavy snowfalls in the area had almost covered the vehicle. A passing motorist alerted rescue services this afternoon.' A wobbly amateur video shot of yellow-clad ambulance officers carrying a blanket-swathed figure in a stretcher up a snowy bank came onto the screen. 'Mr Ballantine was found unconscious near the wreckage, suffering from frostbite, concussion and hypothermia. Doctors at Taumarunui Hospital say it is not known if he has internal injuries. Next, we have an update on the parliamentary debate about our foreign debt. The minister—'

'He said he'd be all right.' Katrien was shaking. 'He had chains and everything. He knew the road—'

Callum switched off the television and took her in his arms. 'Don't upset yourself. He'll probably be quite okay.'

'I should have suggested he stay at the hotel. It was already blowing a blizzard when he left.'

'It may not have happened then. It could have been this morning.'

'No.' She was certain it had happened as he drove away from the Chateau. From her. 'Frostbite,' she said. 'That means amputation sometimes, doesn't it? Concussion—is he still unconscious? They didn't say!'

'He's a mountaineer. And he's had frostbite before and recovered.'

'He was out there all night. Unconscious, not able to help himself, protect himself. He wasn't wearing mountain gear! Just trousers and a jersey. Unless he had a parka and gloves in the car—do you think—?'

'I think he had the sense to wrap up for the journey. How far was he going?'

'I don't know. He didn't say exactly. He was staying at someone's private lodge on his own. There'd have been no one to raise the alarm.'

'Katie, if you're blaming yourself for this, don't.'

'Blaming myself?' She shook her head, moving away from him. 'No. Although if I'd agreed to—'

'To what?'

She hesitated. 'He said we could have dinner at his friends' lodge—where he was staying. I turned him down and we...arranged that he'd come to the hotel instead.'

'Then he'd have had to drive you back to the hotel, and you might have been with him when he went off the road—or he might still have had the accident on the way back to his friends' place. Dining at the hotel was a much better idea.'

'Yes.' She said it bleakly, knowing that if she'd gone with Zachary to the lodge she wouldn't have left it until morning.

'Well, it may be selfish, but I'm glad you weren't with

him.' Callum took her hand again. He looked down at it. 'You were tempted, is that it?'

'Oh, what does that matter?' She snatched her hand away and stood up, unable to sit still. 'What if he dies? What if he loses a foot—or a leg? Both legs? How would he survive that? He lives for his climbing!'

Callum stood up too. For once he seemed at a loss. He shoved both hands into his pockets and stared at the floor. 'It probably won't come to that,' he said finally. 'What's this all about really, Katie?'

She looked at him and tried to see things from his point of view, and was wrenchingly sorry. 'It's about the man who saved my life,' she said. 'And who may be about to lose his.'

Callum pursed his lips as if thinking deeply, then nodded. 'Right. So what do you want to do about it?'

She stared back at him, her thoughts in turmoil, but one overwhelmed all the rest. She said starkly, oddly grateful to Callum for making her put it into words, 'I want to go to him.'

CHAPTER FIVE

'ARE you a relative, Miss Cromwell?' The nurse had recognised Katrien before she'd even given her name, and was eyeing her with covert curiosity.

'I'm a friend. Zachary doesn't have any relatives in New Zealand,' Katrien said. 'His brother lives in England.'

The nurse looked suddenly alert. 'Do you have an address for his brother?'

'I'm sorry, no.'

'Well...we usually only allow relatives—'

'Please—Zachary was with me, the night before the accident.'

'Oh—I see.' The woman still hesitated. 'I suppose, if you're his girlfriend...'

Katrien clamped her lips shut and didn't contradict her. If this was the only way they would let her in she wasn't going to jeopardise her chances.

'I'll ask,' the nurse offered at last. 'Just wait here.' She disappeared through a doorway.

Ask who? Zachary? Was he conscious?

No, or they would have been able to get his brother's address from him.

Katrien waited, gripping her hands together.

In a few minutes the nurse appeared again. 'I'll take you to the intensive care unit.'

'*Thank* you!' Katrien almost fainted with relief.

He was in a big, darkened room with several others. Electronic screens glowed above the beds and in the hush she could hear the rhythmic whisper and muted beeps of the machines. Two nurses enveloped in green robes bent over one of the patients.

Zachary lay on a high white bed, tubes snaking from his nose and arms and wires from plastic patches on his bare chest. He had a nasty bruised cut over one eyebrow, a raw abrasion on his cheekbone, and other bruises on his shoulder and over his ribs. A towel covered his lower body. His left ankle was heavily bound in an elastic bandage and both his feet, elevated on a stack of pillows, were swathed in gauze.

'They'll be all right,' the nurse said, following Katrien's apprehensive gaze. 'We're a bit worried about his hands.' They too were loosely bandaged and raised. 'Frostbite this severe usually only occurs at higher altitudes.'

'He had no gloves?'

'Wet ones—that can make it worse. And also he's had frostbite before, so he's more susceptible to getting it again.' The nurse drew up a chair for Katrien.

'He hasn't woken?'

The woman shook her head. 'Not yet.'

Katrien sank down onto the chair and tentatively laid a hand on Zachary's arm. It was reassuringly warm. She looked at his swaddled hands and felt her eyes prickle with tears. He looked so vulnerable, almost naked to her gaze and yet oblivious of it. Her throat ached. Maybe she had no right to be here. But there was no one else by his side.

'Talk to him,' the nurse advised, adjusting the flow from one of the tubes. 'Sometimes it helps.' She gave Katrien a reassuring smile and quietly went away.

'Zachary,' Katrien whispered, leaning close to his ear. 'Zachary, please wake up.'

She stroked his arm, willing a response from him. 'Your feet are going to be all right,' she said quietly.

How bad was the head injury? Concussion, they'd said on the news. But if he was still unconscious…

She looked around, but the nurse had vanished and the others were still busy. 'You must get better,' she urged, turning again to the man on the bed. 'Please, Zachary. Don't leave me.'

Don't leave me. Clinging to him, coming out of the water, her hands locked around his neck, her cheek against his wet skin while other hands tried to prise her away. Her eyes had been blurred with tears.

They were again. She gritted her teeth and put the palm of her hand on his chest between the plastic patches and said fiercely, 'I've only just found you! You can't die now, damn you!'

You can't die on me, damn it! The echo of his voice, rough with exertion, and the slick, hard surfboard under her cheek, his hands turning her limp body so that her arms trailed in the water as his mouth covered hers.

'You wouldn't let me die,' she told him. 'I won't let *you*. I won't. Do you hear me, Zachary? I won't let you die!'

There wasn't a flicker of response. Angrily, she dashed the salty moisture away from her eyes. Tears were no help to him. 'You want to climb again, don't you?' she said, forcing her voice to calm. 'And you will. I know how much you love the mountains. You took me up there, remember? You wanted to show me…'

She went on talking, reminding him of the places he'd been, the memories they'd exchanged over that fateful dinner, the fun they'd had on the slopes of Ruapehu. Randomly talking, talking. It was like talking to herself.

'That's the idea.' The nurse's approving voice made her jump. 'Can I get you a cup of coffee?'

'Thank you. Black, no sugar.'

The woman checked the monitor and tubes and nodded, then whisked away. When she returned there was another woman with her. A young woman, pale and worried, wrapped in a padded jacket over trousers and a jersey, her blonde hair tied back. Ben Storey's widow.

'I guess you two know each other,' the nurse said, handing a plastic foam cup to Katrien. 'Excuse me.' She hurried away to join one of the other nurses who was signalling to her.

'I'm Wendy Storey.' The blonde woman withdrew her shocked gaze from the unconscious man on the bed and held out her hand.

'I know.' Katrien transferred the cup to her left hand to return the greeting. 'I'm—'

'You're Katrien Cromwell, I know.' Her smile held a trace of humour as she echoed Kate's phrase.

Did Zachary tell her about me? Katrien wondered. But Wendy Storey's next words denied it. 'The model,' she said as she shook off her jacket. 'I didn't know you and Zachary were...friends.'

'We...I was at Ruapehu all this week. We skied together, and had dinner at the Chateau before the accident.'

'I see.' Wendy gave her a frankly enquiring stare, and returned her gaze to Zachary. 'Poor old possum,' she murmured, and patted his bare thigh.

It seemed such a casually intimate gesture. For a second Katrien was consumed with stark, piercing jealousy.

She had no right, of course. No right to even be here, except her own inward conviction that it was where she belonged, a crazy belief that Zachary needed her. 'Here,' she said, standing up. 'You have the chair.'

Wendy protested mildly, but Katrien explained, 'The nurse said talk to him. He hasn't responded to me. Maybe he will to you.'

The other woman nodded. 'Have a break. I'll stay

with him until you come back. You are planning to be here for a while?'

'Yes. As long as it takes.'

It was what she'd told Callum when he'd asked how long she expected to remain at a stranger's bedside.

And then he'd asked her what good she thought she could do.

'I don't know,' she'd replied. 'But I have to be there.'

She hadn't expected him to understand. She still wore his ring, but she realised that this was going to put a strain on their relationship that might prove to be intolerable. Many men would have torn the ring from her finger and stalked out of her life at the first suggestion that she fly to the side of another man, no matter how badly that man was injured.

Callum had been angry and uncomprehending, and when he'd finally left her flat last night his kiss had been clumsy and perfunctory, and she wasn't sure if he'd thought she wouldn't welcome it, or was too annoyed with her to kiss her properly. She had never been able to gauge Callum's feelings as accurately as he read hers.

Wendy was leaning over Zachary, her hand lightly massaging his shoulder.

'Here.' Katrien offered her the coffee. 'I haven't touched it. I can get some more for myself. Or I could bring you one with milk, sugar?'

Wendy took the cup. 'This is fine, thanks.' She turned back to Zachary.

Katrien tracked down a visitors' toilet and rinsed her face in icy water. Supposing she ought to eat something, she followed a sign to a cafeteria, but the overwhelming smell of food was too much. She bought a couple of sandwiches and another cup of coffee, made her way outside and found a seat under a leafless tree in a patch of lawn.

The sandwiches tasted like cardboard but she forced them down. At least the coffee was hot.

She stuffed the sandwich wrapping into the empty disposable cup and lobbed them into a nearby rubbish container. A sickly sun struggled through the bare branches overhead and she lifted her face to it, closing her eyes. She'd had very little sleep and made two long journeys in the last twenty-four hours. And she'd been talking non-stop to an unresponsive audience of one for what seemed like years. Exhausted, she dropped off into a light doze.

She woke with a jerk when her body began to slip down on the hard wooden seat. Foggily, she looked about and ran a hand over her face, then stood up and made her way back to the hospital's main entrance. The grass seemed like sponge underfoot, and her head floated.

A man and woman stood at the entrance, looking about them. The woman held a microphone and the man had a video camera over his shoulder. What were TV people doing here?

'Ms Cromwell?' The woman stepped forward with the microphone. 'We understand you've been keeping watch at Zachary Ballantine's bedside.'

'How do you know that?'

Ignoring the question, the reporter asked, 'How is he?'

'He's unconscious.'

'He hasn't responded to you at all?' The woman's eyes were sympathetic.

'He's not responding to anyone.' She shouldn't be answering these questions, Katrien realised. Trained to react positively to the media, not to show signs of temperament at even the most crass questions, she tried to repair the damage. Making her voice firm and pleasant, she said, 'Really, I'm not qualified to tell you anything.'

'How long have you two been seeing each other?'

Seeing each other? 'Where did you get your information?' she asked. 'We're not—'

'You told the hospital authorities you're Zachary Ballantine's girlfriend.'

'They had no right to tell you that!' she said sharply. Someone must have gossiped. But if she specifically denied it, would the hospital refuse to let her see Zachary again? She had only been allowed in because they thought she was.

'How long have you known each other?' the reporter persisted. 'Where did you meet?'

Maybe she could put them off the scent. 'I...I've known him since I was fourteen,' she said. 'We're old friends.'

The camera operator moved in for a close shot, and she put out a hand to ward him off, turning her face away. 'Please—'

'Is that an engagement ring?' the reporter asked.

'Yes. But it's not—' If she told them it wasn't Zachary's, that she was engaged to another man, that would kill the 'girlfriend' story...or simply intrigue them further and bring more press people sniffing round the hospital, perhaps. The authorities wouldn't like that, and if she admitted she had no real place in Zachary's life they'd ban her from seeing him. 'No,' she said, much too late. And then thought with a sick lurch of her stomach that if Callum saw that denial he'd be justifiably hurt and furious. 'This is private,' she pleaded. 'Zachary Ballantine and I are not officially engaged.'

Even as she said it, she knew she'd probably only made things worse. It would have been wiser to say nothing at all. 'I'm sorry, I have to go.' Pushing past them, she made her way inside the building, and discovered she was trembling.

Surreptitiously she removed the ring from her finger and slipped it into her bag. Too late, of course, but the disastrous encounter outside made her realise that others too had probably assumed it was Zachary's ring. In her present ambiguous situation, it seemed wrong to keep wearing it, almost false pretences.

It was a kind of relief to enter the eerie, hushed world of the intensive care unit again. Another nurse let her in and said, 'There's no change. Mrs Storey is still with him.'

Wendy smiled at her when the nurse led Katrien to the bed and found a second chair. She was stroking Zachary's hair, dark and strangely lank, back from his forehead. 'Hi,' she said. 'Want to change places?'

Katrien shook her head. She envied the other woman's ease with Zachary. Her own claim to an old friendship weighed on her conscience. 'There are TV people outside,' she muttered. 'I…might have put my foot in it.'

Wendy nodded. 'Easy to do. They tend to put words in your mouth, or edit them into something different.' She turned back to Zachary. 'The girls send their love,' she told him quietly. 'I told you that already, didn't I? I couldn't bring them with me. Stacey has to go to school and Yasmin's too much of a handful. Anyway, they wouldn't allow children in here. Get better soon and you can come and visit us, okay? They need to know you're all right.'

She turned to Katrien, her eyes shadowed. 'They were upset about me leaving them,' she whispered. 'Since Ben died they're so scared. Of course I had to come, for Zach. I tried to explain, but I didn't like to tell them how badly hurt he was, because…'

Because she didn't want to frighten them further. Katrien made a sympathetic sound.

'I'll phone them when Stacey gets home from school.'

Wendy returned to stroking Zachary's hair. 'God, I hope he's going to come out of this. I don't think I can bear to lose him too.' She lifted a hand to her eyes.

Katrien put an arm about her shoulders and shared her tears.

They shared a lot over the next hours, taking turns to go and freshen up, or grab a quick meal. And they talked—sometimes to Zachary's still form, sometimes to each other.

'You've known him a long time, haven't you?' Katrien commented at one point, her eyes on the man on the bed, alert for any flicker of life apart from the steady rise and fall of his chest.

'Longer than I knew Ben,' Wendy agreed. 'It was Zach who introduced us.' She chuckled. 'It was always a joke between the three of us, how Ben filched me from right under Zachary's nose.'

'You were going out with him?'

'Oh, casually. But Ben and I took one look at each other and knew that was it.' Her voice became husky.

Inexplicably, Katrien was outraged. Swallowing the emotion, she said evenly, 'Didn't Zachary mind?'

'Ben agonised about that, although I told him that Zachary and I only had a casual relationship—he was always wary of intimacy with women anyway. We were friends, not lovers. And I also told Ben it was no use being noble and self-sacrificing, because although I liked Zach enormously, after meeting Ben I knew there was no other man for me. Still, Ben insisted on a big confession scene, and Zachary just laughed at him and wished us luck. He was best man at our wedding.' She reached out and touched his face, her hand lingering. 'Come on, Zach, come back to us.' She sighed and let her hand fall.

*   *   *

'The girls are fretting,' Wendy worried, returning from another phone call to her mother and children the following day. 'I hate the thought of leaving Zachary like this, and yet...' She stood looking down at him, chewing on her lower lip.

'What would Zachary want you to do?' Katrien asked her quietly, seeing her torn between him and her daughters.

Wendy gave her a grateful look. 'He'd say go home,' she admitted. 'But...'

'Then go,' Katrien advised her. 'I'll let you know as soon as there's any change.'

'How long can you stay?' Wendy murmured.

'Just as long as I'm needed.' She had contacted her agent and said she wasn't available until further notice. Determinedly she pushed the thought of Callum from her mind.

'I bought a paper,' Wendy said. 'You might want to read it. And apparently it was on the TV news last night.'

'It', Katrien discovered after Wendy had left to arrange a flight to her home in the South Island, was an article about Zachary's 'fight for life' and the bedside vigil of his fiancée, 'international model Katrien Cromwell'. Their 'secret engagement', the writer announced gleefully, had been confirmed by Ms Cromwell.

'Oh, no!' she breathed, hastily closing the pages as though she could hide the story from the world.

Callum. She had to get in touch with Callum. She hadn't even phoned him since she'd come racing down here to be with Zachary. Conscience smote her. She should have warned him. It was too much to hope that he'd missed both the TV report and the newspapers—what on earth must he be thinking?

She got up hesitantly. How much could she explain in those circumstances? But she had to try.

Reluctantly, she buttonholed a nurse. 'I have to leave for a little while.'

'Okay,' the woman smiled. 'We'll keep an eye on him.' They all knew her now.

She had to phone Callum at work, from a phone in the public lobby. He sounded distant, guarded. Understandably, she thought.

'I was waylaid by a reporter,' she said, trying to pitch her voice so that it was audible to him without being heard by the entire shifting population of the lobby. 'I shouldn't have spoken to her at all—what I said was wildly misunderstood.'

'I saw the TV report,' he told her.

Katrien closed her eyes. 'You know how the media are. They got it all wrong.'

'One has to wonder,' he said in measured tones, 'how you managed to get engaged to a man in a coma. Especially since I was under the impression that you were engaged to me.'

'I *am* engaged to you!' she said hurriedly. 'It was your ring that…that gave them the wrong idea.' The ring she was no longer wearing, that she had removed too late to prevent this debacle.

'I rather thought it was the fact that you're keeping devoted vigil at the bedside of the injured hero, according to the news reports.'

Katrien winced. 'They're jumping to conclusions—'

'Not unreasonable ones, in the circumstances. When are you coming home, Katie?'

'I have no idea. Zachary's still unconscious.'

Callum's sigh was exaggerated. 'Well, let me know when you're ready to be my fiancée again. I have to go, I'm afraid. I'm keeping a client waiting.'

She didn't blame him for being short with her. He'd already been more patient than ninety-nine per cent of men probably would have been. But she felt very depressed and alone as she put down the phone.

What did you expect? she asked herself scornfully, retracing her steps, stopping on the way for a cup of coffee. Support from the man you left behind to be with someone else? Get real.

Curtains were drawn around Zachary's bed when she returned, and her heart nearly stopped, but one of the nurses emerged, giving her a cheerful smile as she pushed back the curtain.

There was a strong aroma of surgical spirit in the air, and another nurse was preparing to wrap Zachary's hands in fresh lengths of gauze. At the sight of the grossly swollen and blistered purple claws, Katrien swallowed, trying to hide her sympathetic horror, and transferred her gaze to Zachary's face.

They had removed the tube from his nose, leaving his face naked in his unnatural sleep. He was unshaven and his eyes were hidden under closed lids, the long dark lashes unmoving, his mouth slightly parted and the lips cracked. But he still looked wonderful.

The nurse finished her task and laid his hands back on the white linen, straightening to look down at him. 'Dishy, isn't he?' she said dispassionately. 'You're a lucky woman.' Then, looking embarrassed, she added, 'I mean, I'm sure he'll get over this. He's a tough one.' She leaned over and raised her voice. 'Mr Ballantine, your fiancée's here. How about you wake up and say hello to her?'

There was no reaction. The nurse glanced at the monitor over his head. 'There was a small variation when we were turning him in the bed,' she said. 'We thought maybe...' She moved aside. 'Here, you try.'

Katrien bent over him, one hand on the pillow by his head. Her hair fell around her face. 'Zachary,' she whispered. Her throat closed up. She couldn't speak. He looked so handsome and so vital, as if a touch, a breath would wake him. And yet he was profoundly asleep.

Tears shimmered in her eyes, and one fell on his closed eyelid and slid to his cheek. On impulse she leaned closer and kissed it away, tasted the salt of it, and felt the faint flutter of his eyelid under her trembling lips.

'Zachary?' She lifted her head, looking for the slightest sign of response. 'Zachary!' Driven by a need to force some acknowledgement, some sign of life from him, she leaned down again and deliberately laid her mouth on his roughened lips, kissing him with a desperate passion and praying that this, if nothing else, would get through to him.

His lips were slack and dry and unresponsive, and she was about to draw away, giving up in despair, when she felt a tremor of the warm, parched flesh, the faintest reflexive movement.

She lifted her head again, just a few inches, her eyes searching his face so intently that they ached. 'Zachary.' She touched his mouth with hers again, felt again that infinitesimal response, and this time when she lifted her mouth away she was sure she discerned a slight movement of his lashes.

She sat up a bit and looked at the nurse, who was watching with fascination. The woman's eyes moved to the glowing monitor, and she seemed startled by what she saw there.

Then a sound came from the man on the bed, a whispery groan, and the nurse leaned over and pushed a button on the wall.

Zachary moved his head, only an inch or so, but a

definite movement, and groaned again. His eyelids twitched, showed a brief glimpse of sea-green, and closed again.

'Zachary!' Katrien said urgently. 'Zachary, wake up. Please. *Look at me.*'

His head moved again and he grunted tiredly. His lips worked as if trying to form words. A line of strain appeared between his brows.

'It's all right,' Katrien said. 'You don't have to talk.' She kissed him again, feverishly, terrified in case he slipped back into the black world of unconsciousness. 'Just open your eyes.'

There were other people around the bed. Someone took her arm. The nurse who had been watching said with subdued excitement, 'Talk about your Sleeping Beauty! She woke him with a kiss.'

Katrien ignored the hand on her arm, watching Zachary's face. Watching his eyes open slowly, reluctantly, blink once and then fix on her face. She saw the recognition in them before the pressure on her arm increased and someone said firmly, 'Just stand aside for a wee while, Miss Cromwell. We need to do some checks.'

Dazed, she let herself be led away by a nurse and given a bracing cup of coffee. After a while the small commotion around Zachary's bed diminished, and she was allowed back to see him. 'Don't tire him, though,' they warned. 'He's still very weak.'

When they left her there she didn't know what to say. He had a couple of pillows behind his head now. She stood beside him, and then dropped into a chair so that he didn't need to look up to her.

He turned his head tiredly and surveyed her with dazed eyes. 'I'm dreaming, right?' His voice was a mere thread of sound, the words slurred. 'You're not...not really here at all. And you didn't kiss me. I'm lying out in the bloody snow and hallucinating.'

Katrien tried to smile. 'No. I'm here, and you're in hospital. And...I did kiss you.' She hurried on. 'You've been...asleep, for nearly two days. But you're not dreaming now.'

'I don't...' He seemed to lose what he was going to say. 'I feel as if I've been a long way away.'

'I think you were. We were afraid you weren't going to come back.'

'We...?'

'Wendy was here. She stayed as long as she could, but the girls needed her. She said you'd have told her to go home.'

A shadow crossed his face. 'She worried?'

'Of course she was worried. She said she couldn't bear it if she lost you...'

'Poor Wendy.' His eyes drifted shut, his expression one of grief.

'She said you're to get well and come and visit her and the girls.'

Zachary smiled faintly, and opened his eyes as if it cost him some effort. 'And you...' He frowned then, tried to lift a hand to her, and she reached out swiftly and caught at his wrist. She didn't know if he was aware of the state of his hands. 'Shh,' she soothed. 'Don't try to move yet.'

'You're here,' he said in tones of wonder. 'Don't go 'way.'

'I won't,' she promised. His eyelids were drooping, and she was half afraid that he was slipping back into unconsciousness. She looked about the ward. 'Nurse?'

'Tired,' he whispered.

The nurse came and checked his pulse, lifted an eyelid, making him stir irritably. 'He's okay,' she said. 'Let him sleep. We'll probably be moving him out of here shortly.'

Late in the day they made her go to a hotel and advised her to sleep, promising to let her know if Zachary woke again and asked for her. She phoned Wendy, and then Callum.

Wendy was ecstatic, and Callum reserved, although he said politely that he was glad to hear Zachary was improving.

'I need some sleep,' she told him, grateful that he hadn't demanded to know when she planned to go home. 'I…I'll get in touch again later.'

She was tired, but she had to talk with her family. If her mother and Miranda had seen the news they must be wondering what was going on.

She hadn't contacted them before she left; her mother lived in Whangarei, three hours north of Auckland, and Miranda had a busy life with her husband and children and studying by correspondence for a degree. They were accustomed to her travelling about or even leaving the country at a moment's notice. If there was an emergency the agency always knew where to contact her.

Her mother said, 'I knew the TV people had got it wrong. You'd have told us if you'd broken off your engagement to Callum. And he's such a nice young man.'

'Yes, he is.'

'I didn't know you knew Zachary Ballantine.'

'I didn't until last week, not really. We met on the ski field.'

Her mother laughed. 'Trust the media to make a mountain out of a molehill—or a secret engagement out of a friendly gesture to someone you'd only just met! If anyone asks, I'll tell them what really happened.'

Katrien hesitated. Her head buzzed with tiredness. She

wasn't up to explaining right now, and maybe it was best that she didn't.

'Have you talked to Miranda?' her mother asked. 'She was trying to contact you.'

'No, I haven't spoken to her. I was going to phone her after this.'

'I'll do it. Hotel phone calls are so expensive. And you sound tired, darling. Are you all right?'

'I'm fine. Only Zachary's in a bad way. I've been sitting with him.'

'Doesn't he have anyone of his own?'

'Not in this country.'

'Well, it's kind of you to do it. Now you have a good sleep.'

She did sleep, very soundly, and in the morning she returned to the hospital, first having a long shower and changing into a soft wool dress, brushing her newly washed hair to a shine and applying a light touch of eye make-up and lipstick.

They'd moved Zachary to a single room in a medical ward. The nurse who led her to the room said, 'He's a bit disoriented still. He was very hypothermic when they found him, and he's been bashed about a bit, of course. We assumed at first he'd been thrown clear when the ute crashed, but the police say it looks as though he actually extricated himself from the wreckage before passing out completely.'

'What about his hands?'

'He's in quite a lot of pain, and that's a good sign.'

'A good sign?'

'Dead tissue has no feeling. He needs tender loving care and plenty of optimism. Be positive. A good mental attitude can help the healing process.'

'Has anyone contacted his brother?'

'The police got hold of him, but since Mr Ballantine's

come round and doesn't seem to have developed serious complications from hypothermia, I don't think his brother's planning to come all the way over from England. Here we are. Now, keep his spirits up but don't get him too excited.'

Zachary was newly shaved and wearing hospital pyjamas. His legs were under a blanket, but his feet hung over the edge of a mattress laid on top of another, and his eyes were closed. Away from the dim light of the intensive care suite she could see that his cheeks were hollowed, sallow beneath his tan.

She entered the room quietly, but he opened glazed eyes and watched her cross the room to lay the flowers she'd brought him on the locker by his bed, between a couple of get-well cards. His loosely wrapped hands rested on the smoothed hospital coverlet.

As she made to sit down, he said almost inaudibly, 'Aren't…going…to kiss me?'

Katrien looked into his eyes and saw puzzlement. Hesitantly, she bent and brushed her lips across his, then abruptly withdrew and sat down.

'Thanks for…flowers,' he said with an effort. Even breathing, she guessed, was painful now that he was conscious. She remembered the bruises on his ribs. 'Fros'bite,' he said, his eyelids drooping. 'They said fros'bite.…'

'Your feet are going to be all right.' She touched his arm for a moment, feeling the fine, wiry hairs that dusted the skin.

'You've…been sitting with me. They tell me you were very…faithful.'

'I had the time,' she said, not knowing how to deal with this. She looked away, clasped and unclasped her hands, and finally said, 'I wanted to help.'

'I'm…grateful.' He paused, took a couple of laboured breaths. 'Only a bit…confused.'

'Yes, I—' Where did she start explaining?

'Must be the…hypothermia.' He drew a struggling breath. 'Along with…everything else…seem to be suffering…a bit of amnesia. I love you, Katrien… but…when did we get engaged?'

CHAPTER SIX

I LOVE you. I *love* you, he'd said.

Katrien sat dumbstruck. 'Who—who told you we were engaged?' she finally croaked.

'Everyone...talks...'bout my bcau'ful fiancée...'s all round the hospital...you woke me with...kisses.' He smiled at her, slowly and with apparent effort. 'The...the las' thing I remember,' he said, 'is kissing you... goodbye. Then...dreams.'

Be positive, the nurse had instructed. Keep his spirits up. He'd just said he loved her. How was she going to tell him they weren't engaged at all?

'I wish...I could hoi' your hand,' he whispered, and grimaced down at the white-wrapped paws that lay inert on the coverlet.

Following his gaze, Katrien swallowed.

'You've...seen...?' He lifted them from the blanket and let them fall again. A quick frown creased his forehead, his jaw clenching, and she realised the movement had hurt him. 'Pretty...repulsive.'

'I'm not repulsed, Zachary, just so...so sorry.'

'I might...lose them. Trouble is...had fros'bite before...'

She nodded, a lump in her throat making it impossible to speak for a moment. 'It won't come to that,' she told him.

'If i' does,' he said painfully, 'I won't...hold you to...promise.'

'Promise?'

'Your promise…to marry me. If I'm maimed…I'll understan'…'f you change your mind—'

'Do you think it would make a difference?' she interrupted angrily. 'I wouldn't change my mind! Not for that! How can you even *think* it?'

He closed his eyes, and she saw that his lips were clamped together. 'I jus'…I was…afraid…'

Appalled, she reached out and clasped his wrist. 'I would never do that to you, Zachary. Never!'

A nurse bustled in. 'Feeling better now your fiancée's here?' She beamed at Zachary as he reluctantly opened his eyes, and pushed up his sleeve to apply a blood-pressure cuff to his arm.

Katrien tried not to wince, and Zachary smiled muzzily at her. 'Don' know what I'd do…withou' her,' he murmured, his eyes on Katrien.

The nurse watched the machine and nodded. 'Well, you're a lucky man.'

'I know.'

'There.' The woman undid the cuff and made a note on the chart at the foot of his bed. Turning to Katrien, she whispered, 'He's looking better already. Keep it up.'

As the woman left the room, Zachary said slowly, 'I dreamed of you…out there.' His eyelids drooped. 'Wish you'd kiss me again…know you're real.' He forced the heavy lids to open, looking at her with naked longing.

Katrien caught her breath and got up from the chair, scarcely hesitating before she leaned down and pressed her lips gently to his.

She felt his response, eager and warm, and then he sighed, and as she raised her head she knew he was asleep again.

She walked over to the window, looking blindly out at hospital buildings and a square of green lawn with a solitary tree.

She might not have any right to be here masquerading as Zachary Ballantine's fiancée. But he needed her. There was no way out now. Only what on earth was she going to tell Callum?

'I don't believe this,' he said when she phoned from the hotel that evening to explain that she was staying on a little longer. 'Just how close did you and Ballantine get last week?'

'I've already told you, Callum.'

'Look, you've shown your concern, he's on the mend, isn't he? So now—'

'He's afraid he might lose his hands, Callum.'

There was a short silence. Then Callum said evenly, 'I'm sorry to hear that. But there's nothing you can do about it, is there?'

'The nurses say it's important to keep him cheerful and optimistic.'

'And you've decided it's up to you. Why, Katie? Okay, so he pulled you out of the water when you were a kid. Or so he says.'

'That's not fair, Callum. He never said it, *I* did. He wouldn't even admit it in so many words. He didn't want to talk about it.'

'Katie, you didn't mention this the night we heard him speak at the dinner.'

'I told you before, I wasn't certain then that he was the same man.'

'But now you are?' Callum's voice became patient, indulgent. 'Sometimes you can be amazingly naïve, darling. You're a beautiful, desirable young woman. You tell this man that he's your hero. Of course he didn't want to shatter the illusion, although he was careful not to lie outright, apparently.'

'It wasn't like that! I know it's him. I knew beyond doubt when—'

'When?' Callum prompted.

'We went climbing on the mountain. He…I slipped and he had to haul me up—'

'You were in *danger*?'

'Not really. It was a beginners' climb—'

'If he put you at risk—' Callum began furiously.

'I got a fright, that's all. We were roped, and Zachary knew what he was doing. But that's when everything clicked into place, and I knew—'

'For God's sake, Katie! You nearly drowned when you were at an impressionable age, then some strange man came to the rescue and mysteriously disappeared. Now you have another near-miss—'

'I was quite safe with Zachary—'

'He stopped you from falling, but you just told me you were frightened. You've confused the two events in your mind and convinced yourself that he's the man who saved your life all those years ago.'

'You make me sound neurotic.' Katrien twisted the phone cord round her finger, stilling a tremor of doubt. 'You don't understand.'

'Actually,' Callum said bluntly, 'I'm afraid that I do. I'm tempted to come down there and drag you home by the hair.'

'Callum!'

'You know I wouldn't. I love you, Katie. Don't forget that, will you?'

'I won't forget.' Her lips parted to add the words she knew he was waiting for: *I love you too.* But they wouldn't come. 'Goodnight.'

'He's not so well this morning,' they told her the following day, and Katrien's heart stopped in fright. 'He's developed a fever. We're giving him antibiotics.'

Zachary was sleepy, but the drowsiness in his eyes cleared a little when Katrien entered the room. This time she kissed him without being asked, and felt the heat of his dry lips. There was still a drip in his arm, and a jug sat on the bedside locker alongside a cup with a straw.

She poured him a drink and held the straw to his lips, and afterwards he lay with his eyes half closed and glittering with fever. 'Come closer,' he muttered. 'Please.'

She hitched her chair nearer the bed, and he raised an arm, laying it clumsily about her shoulders.

'Be careful,' she warned him. 'Your hand...'

But his eyes had closed again. He'd dropped off to sleep. She sat watching his face, noting the slight flaring of his nostrils with each breath, the tiny movements of his eyelashes. Carefully she raised her hand and stroked back his hair from his sweat-damp forehead. Then she laid her head against his shoulder and just listened to him breathing.

His arm began to slip and she replaced it on the covers without touching his hand. When he grunted and shifted restlessly in his sleep, his eyelids fluttering, she returned to stroking his hair, soothing him. After a while he quieted and the frown of pain between his brows eased, his mouth curving into a relaxed, remote smile. She wondered what he was dreaming about now.

I dreamed of you, he'd told her, out there. While he lay unconscious in the snow.

For two more days she sat with him, watching his fever recede as the antibiotics did their work, and talking to him when he was awake and lucid. She bought books, remembering his tastes from their conversations on the mountain, and read to him.

When they got him out of bed he had to be pushed in a wheelchair, because his hands couldn't cope with crutches.

At the end of the week she came in to find him sitting in the chair by the bed, staring out of the window. The bandages had gone from his hands, although they were still swollen. 'The doctor's just told me,' he said, 'there's no question of amputation.'

'Zachary, that's wonderful news!' She crossed the room to him, and he stood up clumsily, balanced on his good leg, and wrapped his arms about her, holding her tight. His eyes were clear and bright, and he looked down at her and then bent his head and kissed her.

It was a very satisfying kiss, wild and delicious and urgent, and she returned it without thought, their mutual relief and gladness reflected in its tenderness and passion.

When he raised his head again she was shaken by the unmistakable light of desire in his eyes. 'In case you hadn't noticed,' he said, smiling at her, 'I feel *much* better.'

'Obviously.' She thought of Callum and tried to ease away, but cautiously because of Zachary's hands.

He wouldn't let her. 'Don't leave me,' he murmured, and laid his cheek against hers. 'I've been dreaming about this ever since I left you at the hotel that night. Holding you, kissing you, loving you...'

He turned his head and kissed her again, and although she tried to hold back, his mouth was so persuasive, so gently insistent, that she gave up and kissed him in return.

When he finally tore his mouth again from hers he was breathing more audibly. Groaning, he said in her ear, 'This is torture. I've got to get out of this damned place soon. I need you.'

Alarm bells rang in her mind. Carefully, she put her hands on his arms. 'Let go, Zachary. We...we have to talk.'

Reluctantly he loosed her, but kept one arm about her waist. 'I know. Here, help me to the bed.'

Once there, he pulled her down with him, his arm still about her shoulders.

'The nurses won't approve, will they?'

'Too bad.' He leaned back on the pillows, not removing his arm. 'They're talking about discharging me in a day or two.'

'Where will you go?' He couldn't possibly manage on his own.

For a moment he was silent. 'Wendy said I can stay with her and the girls until I'm properly mobile and get the full use of my hands back.'

'In Christchurch?' Katrien failed to hide the dismay in her voice. 'That's...good of her.'

'Yeah. She's already got her hands full with the two girls. They're great kids, but lively.'

And a household with two lively children probably wasn't the best milieu for him to be recuperating in.

He needed a lot of help, still. He had been eating, clumsily, with his hands gloved in cotton and plastic, but his food had to be cut up first. There were dozens of everyday things he would have enormous difficulty with. 'Isn't it too soon for that? Your hands, and your ankle—'

'Before they send me away I'll be able to use crutches if they're padded up enough.'

Katrien hardly hesitated. What else could she do? 'I have a spare room in my flat,' she said.

'I can't ask you to nursemaid me.' Zachary scowled, looked down at the hand lying in his lap and tried to curl it into a fist.

'Don't,' she said, putting her own hand very gently over the misshapen fingers and peeling skin. 'You'll hurt yourself.'

'I've been told to exercise them. Damn it, I *loathe* being dependent on other people for the simplest thing. I'll have to buy some loose shirts without buttons, and—'

'How are you going to go shopping?' she asked him. 'You can't drive a car, and digging out change for a bus or even a taxi will be difficult. Then there's—'

'All right, all right!' He paused. 'Sorry, I didn't mean to snarl at you.'

'That's okay. So what are your options?'

He thought heavily for a few seconds. 'You don't have to do this,' he said.

'I want to.' But how was she going to explain to Callum? She pushed the thought aside, unwilling to deal with it right now.

'Then thank you,' he said almost humbly, and turned to kiss her again. 'I accept.'

She had half expected Callum to carry out his threat and fly down, if not to drag her back by the hair then at least to insist on a confrontation. But he hadn't contacted her and, cravenly, she had stopped phoning him every night.

There was no way their engagement would survive her bringing Zachary home and installing him in her flat. Callum might be tolerant to a fault, but he was no door-mat, and by any standards she had treated him very badly.

She looked at the phone, but surely that was a coward's way. The least she owed him was to see him face to face and talk to him.

She touched her third finger, missing the ring Callum had placed there. She would offer it back when she saw him, of course. Her heart ached sadly. She did love him, but whatever she felt for Zachary was much more powerful than the comfortable, fuzzy feelings of warmth and mild stirring of sexual response that Callum evoked.

He was so nice, it wasn't fair. And some time she would have to tell Zachary how she had unwittingly deceived him.

She should have told him today. Surely nothing now would send him back to the anteroom of death. He might be shocked, upset, even angry, but she couldn't go on letting him think that he had proposed to her—and that she had agreed to marry him. Could she?

If he knew they weren't engaged after all he would refuse to rely on her help, she was sure. And she desperately wanted to do this for him.

He had never asked again how they came to be engaged, saving her the need to forge an explanation. Maybe he had learned to take the fact for granted, because everyone else had. Or maybe his dreams had provided some kind of answer. I dreamed of you...

'And I of you,' she whispered, turning at last from the telephone and beginning to prepare for bed.

And yet, she realised, since the one night when she'd so vividly and unexpectedly discerned her rescuer's face for the first time, the dreams seemed to have left her. Perhaps seeing him in the flesh had exorcised them.

Katrien rented a car to drive them north to Auckland, and packed her meagre luggage into it before going to the hospital for the last time. Zachary had given her the key of the lodge where he'd been staying, and she'd gone round and collected his clothes. 'Leave the skis and mountain gear,' he'd told her. 'I can pick them up another time.'

At the hospital he looked on wryly from a wheelchair

as she packed his things into a carry bag and lifted it off the bed. He was wearing track pants and a plaid shirt, the sleeves unbuttoned, and a loose jersey. Katrien had spent some time stretching the ribbed ends of the sleeves so that he could pull them over his hands without damaging the tender skin.

The charge nurse placed a list of instructions in Katrien's hand. 'There's a diet sheet in there, and some exercises. Make sure he continues to have plenty of protein and lots of calories, and takes his prescribed vitamins.'

Zachary was frowning as the woman left the room, and Katrien asked, 'What's the matter?'

'My hearing wasn't impaired in the accident.'

Katrien smiled. 'She probably doesn't trust you to follow instructions.' He'd been caught trying to walk with his injured ankle before the doctor had given the go-ahead, and they'd only given him crutches with underarm supports because he'd insisted, despite being told he could hurt himself by putting too much weight on them. He'd floored them all by managing to hobble about his room and across the corridor to the bathroom, but he'd been warned that it wasn't wise to stay on the crutches too long.

The charge nurse had sighed to Katrien, 'He's determined—and of course he's accustomed to pushing his body to extremes in ways most of us never do. But try not to let him overdo things.'

On the long trip to Auckland Zachary was largely silent, watching with unseeing eyes the green countryside populated by sheep and cattle, and the dark patches of bush snuggled into the folds of the hills between the scattered rural townships.

As they reached the outskirts of yet another little town, two Maori children riding bareback on a horse trotted by, and a little later a jogger pounding along the road waved at them. Unsmiling, Zachary lifted a hand in reply, and shifted in his seat, flexing his leg.

'Are you okay?' Katrien asked him.

'Just a bit of cramp.'

Katrien slowed. 'We can stop.'

'I said I'm okay,' he said with a hint of irritation.

She increased their speed again. 'I didn't mean to fuss.'

'You don't fuss. I'm a bad-tempered, ungrateful sod.' He slanted her a rueful smile.

She stopped at the next town, bought a snack and drinks, and drove to a picnic area beside the lazy green reaches of the Waikato river. There was a patch of grass, and Katrien unwrapped the food and placed it on a wooden picnic table while Zachary manoeuvred himself onto the bench seat.

Covertly she watched him pick up a club sandwich on his third attempt and raise it to his mouth. He glanced up and she looked away, biting into her own sandwich.

He said, 'This was thoughtful of you, Katrien. I appreciate your not suggesting a restaurant.'

'This is nicer.'

He smiled at her. 'I think so. Very restful.' He turned and glanced at the water, its glassy surface hardly disturbed by ripples that swept slowly from bank to bank. 'The river doesn't bother you?'

'I wouldn't want to swim, but it doesn't frighten me to look at it.'

'You have tried swimming since...have you?'

'I can't.' She suppressed a shudder. 'I know I should face my fear and get over it. I've been told that often enough...'

He started to reach out and then seemed to remember the state of his hands. 'I won't tell you that,' he promised. 'I know it's not that simple.'

Katrien looked at him gratefully. 'I wouldn't have expected you to understand,' she confessed.

His eyes searched hers. 'Why not?'

'You thrive on fear, surely? It gives you an adrenaline rush.'

His eyes flickered. 'That kind of fear makes you cautious, but there's another kind, the kind that cripples. That sheer, stark terror that blacks out every other emotion and leaves you helpless.'

'Have you felt like that—in your mountains?' She found it hard to believe.

He was silent for a few seconds. 'Not in the mountains,' he said finally. 'No.'

After the accident, she guessed. When he was lying helpless in the snow with frostbitten limbs and thinking he might never climb again. She put out her own hand and gently folded it about his, careful not to apply any pressure. 'You've been lucky,' she assured him. Against her selfish wish to keep him away from any further danger, she said earnestly, 'There's no reason you can't go back to the mountains again—when you're properly healed.'

He looked down at her fingers resting lightly on his, and gave an odd little laugh. 'You're right, of course. Nothing to stop me. It's a...comforting thought.' Carefully he turned his hand and curled the fingers as far as he could to enclose hers. He lifted her hand and kissed it. 'I love you,' he said huskily. 'My guardian angel.'

She tried to smile lightly, to hide the rush of warmth that filled her, and he laughed again softly and released her.

When they had finished eating she gathered the scraps and dropped them in a nearby rubbish bin, and Zachary struggled up from the bench and hobbled a few steps to the river's edge, brushing through a couple of bushy shrubs and ducking under the drooping branches of a willow that was just beginning to show a faint hint of green.

'Come here,' he said quietly.

She went to join him, standing at his side, and saw what he'd been looking at—a grey heron standing motionless on the low bank about ten yards downriver.

As they watched, the bird lifted its long beak and took off into the air, wings silently flapping, its long legs outstretched, and disappeared beyond the trees.

Zachary made to turn, but his crutch had dug a small hole in the soft ground as he leaned on it, and he stumbled a little. Katrien put out her hands to help him, and he lurched against her, his weight pushing her back until she was hard against the solid trunk of the willow, trapped by Zachary's body.

He flung out an arm against the tree, adjusting the crutch to brace himself. 'Did I hurt you?'

'No.' One hand lay against the beating of his heart, the other had slipped about his waist. 'Are you all right?'

'Actually, I'm very much all right.' He smiled at her, and shifted his body subtly, teasingly, against hers.

Her own body was answering the unspoken message of his, her knees going weak, her heart hammering. 'We...we should be getting on,' she whispered.

'My thoughts exactly,' he murmured wickedly, and bent his head to kiss her.

And, God help her, she let him. It seemed so right, standing there under the bare tree while the river flowed silently by. She slid both her arms about him, and revelled in the feel of his body, so warm and solid, pressing against the supple feminine curves of hers. Her lips parted eagerly for him, tacitly inviting his deeper exploration of her mouth.

When at last he lifted his mouth he muttered, 'This is torture—I want to touch you, damn it!' His mouth found the taut skin of her throat, and he groaned. 'At least open your blouse for me, Katrien—please.'

She couldn't deny him. The overgrown shrubs and the thick willow trunk concealed them from the highway. With trembling fingers she undid several buttons, revealing the low-cut bra she wore beneath her shirt, and when his head dipped lower she closed her eyes, dizzy with sensation as his lips nuzzled the soft flesh rising above the lacy cups.

Her breathing became faster, and his was harsh before at last his lips returned to hers, demanding and passionate. When he finally drew away, his voice was raw. 'You're so beautiful, I can't stand having you this close and not being able to make love to you properly.' His gaze swept down, and she saw the glitter in his eyes. 'These blasted hands of mine—I want to tear off your clothes and lie down with you right here and now.'

'We'd be arrested,' Katrien said shakily, her fingers fumbling with the buttons, doing them up. 'It's a public place.'

'We could find a private spot here.' He looked along the tree-lined bank. 'A mossy little nook under the trees. Sound good?'

'Sounds very good,' Katrien admitted longingly. 'But not possible.'

'One day we'll come back here and then we'll find it, okay?' He smiled at her, his eyes full of promises.

One day. If only, she thought. If only he still wanted her when she explained that she had in a sense deceived him about their 'engagement'. In Auckland, she assured herself, she would explain. As soon as the right moment presented itself.

Katrien drew up the car in the garage of her flat and got out, opening the door to the hallway before coming back to help Zachary, who had clambered out of the car with his crutches and was eyeing the two shallow steps into the flat with some frustration.

'You'd better lean on me,' she said. The hospital had offered a wheelchair, but Zachary had revolted at the idea, and in her small flat it might have been more of a hindrance than a help.

They negotiated the steps and he said, 'I need the bathroom.'

She handed him his crutches and took him to the bathroom door and he got himself into the room and pushed the door almost shut. Katrien went to fetch the bags from the car.

When he came out of the bathroom she ushered him into the spare bedroom next door. 'The bed's made up,' she said. 'I've switched on the electric blanket to make sure it's aired. Towels are in the hall cupboard. Help yourself. I'll leave the door ajar.'

She'd been advised to let him do as much for himself as possible. And from the way he tensed up when anyone offered aid she knew he was heartily in favour of that principle.

He sat down on the bed, holding his crutches.

Katrien had put his bag on a chair near the bed, and she bent to slide back the zip. 'I can put your things in a drawer and move it onto a chair so you don't have to root round in your bag every time you want something.'

'Thanks.' He bit off the word. 'Maybe later.'

'Zachary,' she said softly, 'it's not so different from accepting help from your climbing partners, you know. You told me it's no big deal, helping each other out when someone gets into trouble. You'd do the same for...anyone. Wouldn't you?'

He looked at her, and his taut expression relaxed a little. 'I don't deserve a woman like you. I'll try to accept help more...graciously.'

She smiled at him, and on impulse laid a hand briefly against his cheek. 'It won't be for long.'

'I keep telling myself if anyone should count their blessings it's me. I still have both legs, both hands...and you.'

She stepped back. 'I'll have to buy some groceries,' she said, 'but I won't be long. You can settle in while I'm gone, have a lie-down, maybe.'

She inspected the refrigerator and kitchen cupboards, made a short mental list, and went back to the car. It wasn't very far to the nearest block of suburban shops, and she made her purchases quickly. Protein and calories, she recalled, placing a sugar-dusted, plastic-wrapped apple strudel on top of the other things in the wire basket.

When she got back to the flat there was a car outside. Her heart plummeted as she recognised it. She'd planned to phone Callum to arrange a meeting the first chance she got—from her bedroom, with the door shut and preferably after Zachary had gone to sleep.

But he was here. As she entered the little hallway with her grocery bags she could hear the two men's voices, but when she closed the door behind her they abruptly stopped.

A moment later Callum appeared in the doorway of the sitting room.

'You're home.'

'I'll be right with you. I have to put the ice cream away before it melts.' Katrien turned, avoiding his eyes, and went into the kitchen.

She opened the freezer compartment and carefully deposited ice cream, some frozen pies and a packet of frozen peas inside, then shut the door and paused there like an arrant coward. She would have liked to run away. This was going to be the most difficult discussion of her entire life.

Slowly she straightened and walked to the other room, head high and shoulders back, to meet two pairs of accusing masculine eyes.

Callum was near the door, his hands thrust into the pockets of his trousers, bunching up his tweed jacket, and his sandy brows meeting in a ferocious scowl.

Zachary stood by the window that looked out on the tree-lined street. He leaned heavily on his crutches, two lines raked between his black brows, his mouth set uncompromisingly and his face pale. She looked at him with a flutter of anxiety, thinking, He shouldn't be standing. It's hurting him.

She parted her lips to ask him if he needed a painkiller, but the cold anger in his eyes stopped her. Then Callum said, 'What's this all about, Katie?'

She forced her gaze away from Zachary. 'I was going to phone you,' she assured Callum apologetically, 'as soon as I could. How did you know we...I was home?'

'I didn't know—since you didn't bother to tell me you were planning to return. I just came by to check on your flat in your...prolonged absence. And seeing the light on, I naturally investigated.'

Katrien blinked. 'You've never done that before... have you?'

'I didn't think it was my place to, before.' Before they got engaged, he meant.

'Well, it was...thoughtful of you,' she said lamely. 'And I'm sorry I wasn't here. We...only arrived a little while ago. I had to buy some food before the shops closed.' Turning to the silent, dark man across the room, she added, 'I didn't expect him to come round.'

'Obviously.' His tone made her heart sink. It was hard and very even. And quite emotionless. 'Callum and I have been having an interesting discussion,' he told her. 'So...would you like to enlighten us both, and tell us which one of us is your fiancé?'

CHAPTER SEVEN

FOR a crazy moment Katrien wanted to say, Both of you.
But as she stood in anguished silence Callum said to
Zachary, 'I just told you—she's still engaged to me.
Some reporter made a stupid mistake, and Katrien got
the idea into her head that a denial would affect your
recovery.'

Zachary seemed to be ignoring him. 'Katrien?' he
pressed quietly.

She swallowed. 'There's some truth—'

Again Callum interrupted. 'For God's sake, man—
you were at death's door. She was *sorry* for you! It's
my ring she's wearing!' He was two steps from Katrien,
and he covered the space between them and seized her
left hand even as she instinctively tried to whip it behind
her back. 'Or was...'

Katrien wrenched her gaze from Zachary's stony expression to Callum's aggrieved one. 'I thought you'd
want it back, after...what I've done to you.'

He dropped her hand and looked at her broodingly. 'I
won't say it hadn't crossed my mind,' he acknowledged
stiffly. 'But I know it's your soft heart that's got you
into this silly fix.'

'Callum, I'm sorry—'

'This is very touching,' Zachary cut in, 'but I think
you owe it to me to answer my question yourself,
Katrien.'

If anything, he looked paler than before. Alarmed, she
moved towards him. 'Zachary, please sit down.'

'I don't want to sit down!' he said harshly. 'Just answer the damned question. Did you ever agree to marry me?'

Her lips trembling, she opened her mouth, casting around for some less brutal way to tell the truth. There wasn't one. 'No,' she said finally. 'You never asked me.'

The faintest flicker of expression crossed his hard features, as if he'd inwardly flinched. 'I see.'

She felt as though she'd hit him. 'I don't think you do. But I'm…sorry for deceiving you. It was… The situation was difficult. I'd like to explain later.' She glanced at Callum. She could hardly pour it all out in front of him.

'No explanations are necessary.' Zachary moved at last, lurching towards the door, brushing past them. 'You two have some talking to do, no doubt. I'll leave you to it while I go and pack.'

'Pack?' Katrien swung round to follow him. 'You can't!'

His head turned, and she recoiled from the fury in his face, his voice. 'I'm not totally helpless!'

'I mean, you can't just leave! Where will you go?'

'I'll find somewhere.' As she made to catch at his arm, he said with something like loathing, 'Don't touch me, Katrien! I won't be responsible for what I might do.'

'Zachary, we need to talk—'

'Frankly, I don't think I ever want to speak to you again. Go and talk to your *fiancé*.'

She stood shivering while he made his halting way into the spare bedroom, pushing the door almost shut.

Katrien stood torturing her lower lip for a second or two, then went into her own room and rummaged in her handbag for Callum's ring before returning to the sitting room.

'Callum,' she said hesitantly, holding the tiny circlet with its glittering stones out to him, 'I've been an awful fool about this, and I'm truly sorry. You didn't deserve to be treated this way. But...I can't marry you now.'

He looked at the ring without making any attempt to touch it. 'Maybe we both need to think things over,' he suggested gruffly.

'I don't believe that would do much good.'

'I love you, Katie. You told me you loved me.'

'I thought I did. I do, but not...not in the way you deserve. I don't feel...'

'You don't feel the way you do about *him*.' Callum jerked his head towards the spare room. 'You think you're in love with him, don't you?'

She shied away from admitting it even to herself. Her emotions—and her life—were too convoluted right now to allow her to get a handle on that possibility. 'I...don't know,' she said. 'All I wanted was to help him. I had to be there for him.' Nothing else had been as important as that.

Callum's lips tightened, then he shook his head almost pityingly. 'You're fixated on the man. You've built up this image of some great hero in your mind, based on an incident that you barely remember. I could very nearly feel sorry for him—if he ever falls from that pedestal you've got him on it's going to be a hell of a long way down.'

'Take your ring, Callum—please. I can only apologise again, and hope you find someone who's a better person than I am.'

Looking stubborn, he reluctantly took the ring from her hand and slipped it into a pocket. 'I'll never love anyone as I love you,' he said, bringing tears of guilt and misery to her eyes.

He grabbed at her shoulders and dragged her close to him, his mouth coming down on hers in a desperate kiss.

'When you come to your senses,' he said, releasing her at last, 'get in touch. I'll be waiting.'

He strode to the hallway and let himself out of the front door, banging it behind him. Katrien wiped the shimmering tears from her eyes and scrubbed at her wet cheeks with her palm. It was only then that she saw the shadowy figure in the doorway of the spare room. How long had Zachary been standing there?

He came forward haltingly, an indexed address book in one hand making it difficult to manage his crutches. 'I'll use your phone, if I may?' he asked with chilly formality.

'Of cour... No,' she amended. 'I mean, why?'

He explained with insulting clarity, 'To phone a friend and beg a bed for the night. Tomorrow I'll fly down to Christchurch and stay with Wendy for a while.'

'You said she already had her hands full.'

His mouth compressed. 'I don't have a choice any more.' He looked about the room, found the telephone sitting on the folded-down antique desk and limped over to it. He propped the crutches against the front of the desk, glanced at the book, then picked up the portable handpiece, trying to hold the address book open with his other hand.

'This isn't necessary,' Katrien said. 'There's no reason for you to leave.'

Zachary raised his brows ironically.

She hesitated. 'Callum and I...we're not engaged any more.'

'I'm sorry to hear it,' he said remotely. 'That's why you were crying?'

'No...yes.' She pushed back her hair impatiently. 'It's complicated,' she muttered.

'Complications seem to be your specialty.' Under the even tones she knew he was searingly angry. As if to confirm it, he went on, 'In case there's any doubt in your mind, let me assure you that I have no intention of holding you to your supposed engagement to me, either.'

'I never told anyone we were engaged,' she defended herself. 'It was a misunderstanding.'

'Which you didn't attempt to correct.'

'The hospital staff said it was important to keep your spirits up.'

'By pretending a relationship that didn't exist?'

'You didn't mind at the time. If you'd asked me outright I'd have told you the truth, once you were well enough.'

'I did ask once. I thought you were hurt that I didn't remember. So like a sensitive 'new age guy' I decided I should leave it, hoping my memory would return in due course and let me recall how we'd managed to get engaged between dinner and whatever happened to me on that road.' He paused again. 'I was easily fooled, wasn't I?' he said dispassionately.

'It wasn't my intention. Things just…happened.'

'You mean you just happened to be in Taumarunui, and just happened to wander by the intensive care unit, and just happened to see me there?'

Katrien flushed at his over-polite tone. 'When I heard about the accident I flew straight down and asked to see you. If they hadn't thought I was your girlfriend I don't think I'd have been allowed in. So I let them think it. And then a reporter saw my—Callum's—ring and jumped to conclusions. After that the whole thing snowballed and I just couldn't stop it.'

He nodded. 'I understand.'

'You do?' she asked with eager hope.

'You acted out of the goodness of your heart,' he said on a sarcastic note.

'Callum's wrong. It wasn't just because I was sorry for you.'

He looked at her for a moment, weighing her answer. 'No, you had some misguided idea that you owed me something.' His mouth curled with distinct aversion.

'I do owe—'

'Oh, for God's sake, Katrien!' He made a slashing movement of repudiation with his free hand. 'Spare me your gratitude, will you? I don't *want* it.'

'I know, but I can't help—'

'If you ever owed me anything,' he said angrily, 'you've more than repaid the debt. Consider it cancelled.'

'I've hurt you,' she said in a low voice. 'The last thing I wanted—'

'Hurt?' His head went up. Then he laughed, a harsh, cruel sound. 'You flatter yourself. Oh, I grant you're a stunner, and of course it boosted my ego when I thought you'd chosen to accept my proposal. But at the same time I figured I must have been out of my mind when I'd made it.'

He might just as well have slapped her. Hard. 'You told me you loved me,' Katrien reminded him, her throat raw.

'It seemed to be expected,' he said coolly. 'A man who's about to confess he doesn't remember asking his supposed fiancée to marry him had better preface the confession with a declaration of love, I thought. As a matter of interest, how long were you planning to keep up this charade?'

Katrien was beginning to be angry herself. 'I just wanted to help. I would have told you—'

'When?'

'When you didn't need me any more.'

She saw his whole body stiffen. 'I don't need you. I

never did. I believe I recall indicating once that there wasn't room in my life for a woman on a permanent basis.'

'I hadn't forgotten.'

'Good. Then you'll understand that I'm relieved to find I'm not expected to settle down to wedded bliss with you after all.'

Having effectively silenced her, Zachary returned his attention to the telephone in his swollen fingers. He had to look at the address book again, and then he started painstakingly pushing the tiny buttons. She heard faintly the tinny sound of the signal that meant he'd taken too long to dial. He swore under his breath and started again.

It was unbearable to watch. Defeated by his helplessness, she said, 'Let me do it for you.' But as she went to his side he said ferociously, 'I don't want your help!' and went on jabbing at the buttons with the end of one misshapen finger.

Wanting to snatch the receiver from him, Katrien retreated to the window and stood there, her arms crossed and her hands absently rubbing at the sleeves of her sweater.

There was no sound behind her, and she turned to see him with the receiver to his ear, listening intently and with growing impatience. Finally he lowered the phone, scowling, pressed the cut-off button, then with obvious difficulty rechecked the address book and began the whole process over again.

Katrien found her hands were gripping hard at her arms.

He gave up and began looking for another number in the address book. As he juggled it with the receiver, the phone fell from his hand to the carpet, and he bent to fumblingly pick it up while Katrien watched impotently. She winced as he stabbed out a number again, surely hurting his damaged fingers. He must have misdialled, because the 'no such number' tones began once more and he swore again, loud and viciously, hurling the portable receiver across the room. It hit a wall and fell to the carpet.

Zachary stood with his hands curled into ungainly fists, his face a study in useless fury.

Katrien walked forward and picked up the telephone receiver.

'I apologise,' he bit out. 'That was stupid and juvenile. Is it damaged?'

'I don't think so.' She went over and replaced it on its cradle, leaving her hand over it as she turned to look up at him. 'Isn't what you're trying to do stupid and juvenile? Cutting off your nose to spite your face? There is absolutely no good reason for you to go anywhere tonight. Or until you're fully recovered.'

He leaned back on the desk, his eyes tightly closed, and lifted a hand to his face, briefly touching his dark brows before he opened his eyes and studied the reddened, distorted fingers only inches away. Then he sighed heavily, defeated. 'All right,' he admitted. 'You win...for now.'

Relieved, Katrien withdrew her hand from the telephone. 'I'll make us some dinner.'

He nodded reluctantly. 'Useless offering to help, of course.'

She supposed it was an olive branch of sorts. 'That's all right. I'll call you when it's ready. You could watch some television, if you like. I'll help you to the sofa.'

'I'm okay.'

He wasn't, she knew. He'd been standing too long and his face was white with pain, but he wouldn't admit it.

When she came to tell him the meal was ready he was

sitting on the two-seater with a magazine open on the square swamp kauri coffee table that she'd brought home from a trip to visit her mother in the north. The wood was thousands of years old and beautifully mottled.

They'd found in the hospital that magazines were easier for Zachary to manage than the smaller pages of a book. He must have taken this one from the stack on the lower shelf of the nearby bookcase.

The kitchen was not large but it was efficiently laid out, and the dining area held a table for two. She had made a creamy soup, followed by curry and rice. The steak she'd bought would keep. When it was cooked she would need to cut it for him, and tonight he was over-sensitive to reminders of his temporary handicap.

He ate in silence, but as he pushed away his empty plate he said in clipped tones, 'That was very good.'

'There's more if you want it.' At least they were talking, even if the conversation lacked sparkle.

He shook his head, and she took their plates to the sink, then placed a generous piece of apple strudel in a bowl, added a scoop of ice cream and poured fresh cream over it. For herself she cut a narrow slice of the strudel and placed it on a flat plate.

When she put them on the table and resumed her seat, he looked from his own plate to hers.

'You need the calories,' she said. 'I can't afford them.' If she followed his recommended diet she'd soon be as big as a house and out of a job.

'This is going to be difficult for you,' he commented, picking up his spoon. 'Surely it can't be healthy to starve yourself?' He surveyed what he could see of her figure, encased in a fine lambswool sweater that gently hugged her breasts and waist.

Katrien shrugged. 'I eat a very healthy diet. And I've never had much of a taste for greasy, fatty foods.'

'This isn't greasy.' He had already taken a mouthful of cream-covered strudel and swallowed it. 'It's delicious.'

'I can't take the credit, I'm afraid.' The meal seemed to have thawed him a bit, the icy anger receding. The way to a man's heart...

She smiled to herself, and he said sharply, 'Something funny?'

'Not particularly. I'm glad you're enjoying your meal.'

She ate her strudel, and got up to make coffee while Zachary finished his.

He had to hold the hot cup in both hands, so she served his in a thick mug. Even so, he put it down quite quickly, and she knew he had to allow it to cool. Biting her tongue, she restrained herself from offering to hold it to his lips. 'I'll go shopping for an insulated cup tomorrow,' she said.

Even that brought a scowl to his face. 'I've had enough anyway.' He pushed back his chair and picked up the crutches he'd propped against the table. 'I can do with an early night after that journey. Will you mind if I take the magazine I was reading to bed with me?'

'Of course I don't mind. I'll bring it into your room. Feel free to borrow any reading matter you like.'

She went and picked up the magazine and took it to his room, tapping on the door even though it was open.

Zachary was sitting on the bed. He had struggled out of the jersey, and the sleeves of his shirt had never been fastened, but she saw at a glance that he wasn't able to manipulate the tiny buttons in front. One of the nurses must have helped him when he'd dressed this morning.

Without speaking, she put the magazine down on the bed and knelt before him. Zachary sat stone-faced and unmoving while she quickly unfastened the shirt, trying to avert her eyes from the taut male torso she'd revealed, not allowing her fingers to touch his skin as they longed to do.

'Tomorrow I'll leave it undone,' he said.

Katrien didn't argue. 'Do you have everything you want?'

He stopped, looking down at her, and the mockingly sensual look he sent her made her blood pound. 'What do you think?' Then he laughed softly. 'Yeah, I'll manage.'

Katrien stood up, making for the door. 'Let me know if there's anything else you need. I mean…' She turned in the doorway.

'I know what you mean.' He sounded tired now. 'Thanks.'

There were messages on her answering machine from several of her friends, her sister, her mother and her agent. Most of them could wait until morning, but she decided to phone Miranda tonight.

'What on earth have you been up to?' her sister demanded. 'Mum said you hardly know Zachary Ballantine, but the media—'

'You know what they're like,' Katrien chided her.

'Yeah, yeah, I know. So you haven't been holding his hand and sponging his fevered brow?'

'I couldn't hold his hand, they're both frostbitten.' But she had sponged his brow more than once when he was tossing and sweating with fever.

'You *were* with him?' Miranda sounded astonished. 'What did Callum say?'

'He…we're not engaged any more.'

Miranda considered that in silence. 'You mean…the reporters were right? You're engaged to Zachary Ballantine?'

Hastily Katrien denied it. 'No. But…I brought him home with me, to my flat. He had nowhere else to go, and Callum came round before I got a chance to explain to him and…well…'

'You had a row and he broke it off.' Miranda took a moment to digest that. 'This mountain climber of yours must be pretty special.'

'He's not mine. I'm just helping out until he can do things for himself. He can barely use his hands.'

'That'll cramp his style a bit.' Miranda laughed.

'It's not like that. Miranda—you remember that time I nearly drowned?'

'I'll never forget it! None of us will.'

'Would you know the man who brought me in if you saw him again?'

'Nobody got a good look at him—you know that. We were all too worried about you.'

'It was him. Zachary.'

'*What?*'

Katrien let her absorb it. 'That's why I'm doing this. He needs my help for a while. But as soon as he's fit again he'll be off. So don't read too much into it, okay?'

After she put down the receiver she wondered if Miranda believed her. She'd sounded sceptical, but had promised to put straight anyone who asked. Wearily, Katrien pushed a wayward strand of hair back from her eyes. Tomorrow she would try to explain to her mother.

She should have anticipated having to explain to her agent too. Hattie Fisher had no conception of private lives for her clients.

'I thought you were engaged to some banker,' the woman said next morning, when Katrien seated herself at the desk in the sitting room and began returning the several calls she'd found on the machine. 'So what's all this about Zachary Ballantine? Why didn't you tell me you had a relationship with him? How long has it been going on?'

'I don't. It hasn't.' Katrien hoped Zachary wasn't within earshot. He'd gone into his room after breakfasting with her in an atmosphere of frigid politeness, but of course he couldn't completely shut the door. 'It was a media mistake.' She didn't want Hattie looking on this as a publicity opportunity.

'Oh, sure. That's why you dropped everything to sit at his bedside. A great job came up last week but I had to give it to someone else. Anyway, now that you're back I have some assignments lined up for you.'

'I can't leave Auckland for a while.'

'Why not? Never mind, you won't need to just yet. Come in and see me today.'

'This afternoon,' Katrien promised. First she had to make sure Zachary had everything he needed.

When he emerged from his room she said, 'You want some shopping done, I know. If you tell me what you need...?'

'Apart from a baby cup?'

'It's not a baby cup. But maybe I should get you one if you're going to sulk like this!'

She regretted the accusation the instant she'd said it, and he looked furious. 'I'm not sulking,' he said frostily.

'Then you're giving a damned good imitation of it. Snide remarks, skulking in your room.'

'I've been doing the exercises the physio gave me.'

Oh, hell. 'I see.' She raised her eyes briefly to the ceiling. 'I'm sorry.'

'Forget it.' He paused. 'I could do with a few things.' Obviously he'd have preferred not to say so.

'I'll get them for you.'

She saw his dislike of the idea. But there was no way he could go shopping for himself.

She asked what he needed besides the loose shirts he'd mentioned, and he said underpants, more track pants and a pair of slippers. 'I have trouble putting socks on,' he explained unemotionally.

The slippers were relatively easy—she found some plain brown ones in the right size with soft linings—but the shirts took longer to find.

An insulated cup was difficult to come by too, and those she finally tracked down had children's cartoon figures on them. She settled for one sporting a teddy bear with a pink bow at its neck.

When she produced it with some trepidation from the shopping bag Zachary's mouth went grim, then he suddenly laughed. 'Coals of fire?'

'It was the only one I could find,' she apologised, relieved at his laughter.

'Oh, what the hell. How much do I owe you? I'll write you a cheque when I can hold a pen properly. And for your other expenses, of course.'

'I won't take money for the cup. It's a present.'

'If I don't pay for it, it's yours.'

So he didn't want gifts from her. 'Okay,' she said, hiding her hurt with a shrug. 'I suppose you won't have much use for it when your hands are healed.'

'There's something else I should have asked you to get for me.'

'Oh, what? I have to see my agent this afternoon— maybe I could get it then.'

'A voice-activated tape recorder.'

'I have one.' She often used it to make verbal notes for her travel articles. 'What do you want it for?' she asked curiously, then bit her lip, half expecting a snub.

'I might as well make some constructive use of my

time if I can,' he answered after a second. 'I thought I might try dictating that book. Maybe the words will come more easily if I'm speaking them. I can't write or type.'

'That's a great idea!' She was genuinely pleased.

'At least it may stop me from going stir-crazy.'

She got her machine and inserted a fresh tape, promising to buy more for him. Zachary thanked her unemotionally. He was being civil, making the best of things, but she knew he was still seething with angry frustration. It was probably just as well she'd promised to see her agent today. If Zachary was going to erupt in some way she'd as soon be out of the line of fire.

'You look tired,' Hattie said critically. 'Nursing the sick doesn't suit you.'

'I only got back last night. Give me a couple of days.'

'This thing with Zachary Ballantine. If it's not an engagement, how serious is it?'

'I already explained—' Katrien stopped at the disbelieving smile she encountered. She didn't want to explain every detail to anyone, and protesting wasn't getting her anywhere. 'It's not serious,' she said. The agent was always on the lookout for ways to get her clients' names in the media, but this time Katrien refused to cooperate. 'Tell me about these assignments. I don't want anything that's going to take me away overnight, though.'

The agent looked knowing, and Katrien said hastily, 'It isn't what you're thinking. Can we just get on with this?'

'Well, I've had several enquiries about you since you made the news. But there's one that's really exciting…'

A big company wanted a 'face' to identify with a new range of toiletries to be marketed in both Australia and

New Zealand, with eventual expansion to other parts of the world. 'It's to be called Snowfire,' Hattie said. 'You have the kind of looks they want. Serene, aloof, sexy.'

She didn't feel at all serene or sexy at the moment. Aloof she might manage, Katrien thought wryly. Maybe she could take lessons from Zachary. That just about summed up how he'd been since last night.

It was the kind of job models dreamed of, representing a major company. Most houses would pay good money for the regular use of a face and name, and even more if they wanted an exclusive contract.

'What are they offering?' she asked.

Even in her present don't-care mood, the suggested sum made her blink.

'It's going to be an expensive promotion,' the agent said. 'TV commercials as well as print ads in magazines and newspapers. And there should be no problem with your ban on swimsuit ads, because they're going for a theme of snow. But the competition for the job will be fierce. And they'll want to see you at some stage.'

'I suppose so. Thanks for suggesting me.'

'We need to be careful about what else you accept in the meantime. Nothing that will clash with their image, or identify you with a rival firm. It's just as well you don't have a lot of other assignments booked just now. I'll tell them, of course, that you're considering other work, being chased by several firms.'

Katrien smiled thinly. Of course.

'Meantime I've got two magazines who want you for their covers. That would help raise your profile without committing you to a lot of time.'

'Cover pictures? When?'

'Not just pictures. Stories. Interviews. You and your mountaineer are a hot couple—waking him with kisses and all that is just made for the women's magazines.'

'I'm not doing it,' Katrien insisted. 'No stories, no interviews.'

Hattie sighed. 'Think of your career, Katrien. We should use this. Being involved with a well-known mountaineer could do you some good with the Snowfire people too. It would fit beautifully with their ad campaign.'

Katrien unclenched her teeth. 'We can't use it. I'm not involved with him. We're just...'

'Good friends?' The agent looked sceptical. 'Yeah, sure you are.'

CHAPTER EIGHT

KATRIEN turned on the shower for Zachary next morning and made breakfast for them both while he was in the bathroom. Afterwards he went back to his room to do the first set of exercises that he would repeat during the day.

He spent much of the day talking into the tape recorder, often with long pauses. Once when she peeked through the half-open door of his room he was dozing. He reluctantly allowed her to do his washing and feed him regular meals, but he kept out of her way as much as possible, and when she drove him to his appointment at an outpatients' clinic for a check a couple of days later, she could see he was progressing nicely.

Katrien's agent phoned to say the Snowfire people wanted her to fly to Sydney for an audition.

'I can't go to Australia right now,' Katrien said just as Zachary came into the room and swung on his crutches over to the coffee table where he'd left one of his tapes.

The agent's voice rose. 'This is the best chance you've ever had. And you're hot at the moment. We can use that to get you an even better deal if they make us an offer. What is the matter with you?'

'Nothing is the matter with me.'

'It's that man of yours, then? Can't he do without you for one day?'

Zachary picked up the tape, dropped it and swore softly, manoeuvring it back into his swollen hand. He still had trouble with small objects.

125

She switched her attention back to the exasperated voice in her ear. 'One day?' she repeated distractedly. She should have taken this call through to her bedroom. Zachary was moving out of the room now, but slowly because of his crutches.

'It's only a three-and-a-half-hour flight. If you leave early in the morning, with the time difference you can spend a full day over there and be back the same night.'

'I'll think about it.'

When she finished the call Zachary came out of his room. 'You're not turning down work on my account, I hope.' He sounded coldly irritated.

She had turned down a couple of things besides the cover stories suggested by the agent. She shrugged. 'Nothing I really wanted to do.'

His mouth straightened. 'If I thought you had I'd leave right now. Somehow. The lady seemed rather agitated. You've got something going in Australia?'

'An audition in Sydney.' She told him about the Snowfire project and he watched her carefully.

'You must go, of course.'

She hesitated. 'I suppose I could leave a couple of cooked meals for you to reheat. You can manage the microwave, can't you?'

Receiving a testy affirmative, she said, 'Anyway, it isn't until next week. By then your hands will have improved still further.'

'You've read all those, haven't you?' Katrien asked, finding Zachary sitting at the coffee table that afternoon with a magazine. 'I'll buy some more.'

'It's okay. I'm trying to find out how real writers do it.' He had the page open at one of her articles. 'This woman, for instance. She's good.'

'Thank you.'

He glanced up blankly, frowned down at the page. Then looked up again, enlightened. 'You're Kate Winston? I should have known. Nearly all these magazines have that name in them.' He sat back, pushing himself into the corner of the sofa. 'There's no end to the surprises you pack, is there?' For some reason he didn't seem terribly pleased. 'How long have you been writing?'

'I scribbled at school—pieces for the school magazine and stuff. My first sale was three years ago. I thought you didn't read travel articles.'

'As you said, those who can't do it read about it. Right now, I can't do it.'

She said, 'I have some books about writing technique in my bedroom. I'll lend them to you.'

'Thanks.' He looked about the room. 'I don't see a typewriter or word processor.'

'I use a laptop computer and a portable printer. I do a lot of my writing in hotel rooms.' At home her computer slid into a drawer of her bedside cabinet, and her most used reference books sat on a shelf below.

Zachary spent the evening reading the books she gave him, his long legs stretched out as he sat on the sofa. Katrien put on one of her favourite CDs, then curled into an armchair with a new novel that she had trouble getting into, because she kept covertly glancing at the silent man a few feet away. She wanted to get up and take the space that stayed temptingly empty beside him, but that would be tantamount to an invitation and she didn't dare risk a rebuff.

Zachary was determined to keep his distance. He wasn't indifferent to her physically, but it didn't mean he wanted her in any other way. Emotionally, he had repudiated her. Supposing she lured him into her bed, she would have only herself to blame if he walked away afterwards and left her without looking back.

At the very thought of going to bed with him, she felt her body go warm, her bones fluid.

Zachary looked up suddenly, and caught her watching him. His eyes darkened, then they narrowed, and his mouth kicked upward in a sardonic little quirk. He closed the book he was reading and struggled to his feet, steadying his injured leg.

She held her breath as he limped towards her, the lids lowered over his eyes. He stopped before her chair.

Katrien tipped her head back, knowing and not caring that her gaze was openly sexual, pleading for a response.

She saw his chest rise and fall under the soft knit cotton of the new V-necked sweatshirt, and the beat of the pulse at the base of his tanned throat. 'Goodnight, Katrien,' he said, and swung away from her, on his way to the door.

She closed her eyes, her hands clenching on the open book.

Next day someone phoned and asked to speak to Zachary. The only other calls for him had been from Wendy Storey, but Katrien handed him the receiver without a thought, and a few minutes later he said curtly, 'No. Sorry. No comment,' banged the phone down and told her it was a journo from a city magazine asking for an interview with them both. 'And we've just given the game away.'

'There isn't any game, is there?' she replied serenely. 'It's hardly a scandal these days for a man and a woman to be sharing a flat.'

That week another magazine flashed its cover with the words 'Mercy-dash Model and Hero of Himalayas in

Love-nest Hideaway'. There was a file picture of Katrien on the cover.

She'd done some work for the magazine previously, and her agent, confronted with the copy Katrien had bought when she saw the billboard at her corner store, told her that yes, the contract did allow them to reuse the picture, provided they paid a residual for it.

'A complaint won't help,' Hattie advised pragmatically. 'No one would believe your denial, and it will just keep the interest going longer.'

She looked almost pleased, and Katrien asked, 'You didn't give them the story, did you?'

'No, but it won't do you any harm.'

Katrien arrived home to find her sister cosily drinking coffee with Zachary.

He seemed more relaxed with Miranda than he ever was around Katrien, smiling and laughing, lounging on the sofa while Miranda poured him more coffee and told Katrien to get herself a cup.

'What have you done with the children?' Katrien asked

'Drowned 'em,' Miranda replied cheerfully. 'No, actually I have to go and fetch them soon. I swap kids once a week with a friend, and normally I'd be swotting for my exam, but I'm playing hookey today to check out your dishy boarder.' She cast a cheeky, flirtatious look in Zachary's direction, and Katrien looked at him anxiously, afraid to see the forbidding, closed expression she so often saw on his face. But he was laughing again, obviously enjoying himself.

A magazine lay on the table among the coffee cups, and Katrien cast her sister a reproachful look.

Miranda looked rueful. 'I just bought it today. I didn't realise Zachary hadn't seen it.'

After Miranda left Katrien said, 'I had nothing to do with that story, and the cover picture is an old one.'

Zachary nodded, his expression inscrutable. 'Will it harm your career?'

Katrien laughed shortly. 'My agent seems to think it might help. She wanted me to give interviews about our…our supposed relationship.'

'I read the article. There's nothing in it, just a lot of innuendo built on the fact that we won't talk to them.'

'I know. All I can do is apologise.'

'No need. I suggest we neither confirm nor deny the story.' He shrugged. 'If it's good for your career, I'm not bothered by it.'

Relieved, she started gathering up the cups and the remains of a chocolate log Miranda had brought along, and Zachary began to help, with slow care.

'I like your sister,' he said.

'She's very happily married.' She wished she hadn't said that. It almost sounded as if she was warning him off, and that was ridiculous. 'Her husband's nice too.'

He cast her a slightly amused look. 'So I gather.' A cup began to tip from the pile he was trying to carry, and they both made an attempt to rescue it. But it evaded their hands and fell to the pale carpet, spilling the dregs that remained in the bottom.

'Damn, damn, *damn it*!' Zachary swore, his mood abruptly changing. He banged the remainder of the heap of crockery down onto the coffee table.

'It doesn't matter. It'll sponge out easily.'

'That's not the point!' He was furious with himself.

'I know.' She put her hands over his, unable to stop herself offering unwanted comfort. 'But it won't be for ever. They're almost back to normal.'

He closed his eyes and in a goaded voice said, 'I told you, *don't touch me*, Katrien!'

She whipped her hands away, stepping back from him. 'I'm sorry.'

'No.' He opened his eyes. '*I'm* sorry. You've been infinitely patient and I'm like a bear with a sore head. Or sore paws, as they say in America.' He lifted his hands wryly.

Zachary was adept with one crutch now, and his hands were almost healed. But the day before Katrien was due to fly to Sydney for the Snowfire audition, he tripped coming out of the bathroom and wrenched his injured ankle.

Katrien, just out of bed, heard him fall and raced into the hallway in her nightgown, dropping to her knees beside him. 'Zachary! What have you done?'

He was cursing savagely, but abruptly stopped and clamped his mouth tight. She saw that his complexion had gone sallow, and his forehead was damp with sweat. 'I'm all right,' he said. 'Give me the damned crutch.'

But he couldn't put any weight on the ankle at all, swearing again when he tried, and she had to help him into his bedroom, where he collapsed awkwardly onto the mattress, Katrien falling with him, sprawled across his body with her arm pinned under him.

He had closed his eyes, and his face was so pale she thought he'd fainted. She raised her free hand and brushed his hair away from his damp forehead, and he opened his eyes.

They looked glazed, and as she peered anxiously at him, the pupils enlarged and darkened. 'God, Katrien,' he muttered. 'Do you have to...?' Something like anguish flitted across his face. Colour came into his taut cheeks, and his eyes wandered from her face to the gaping neckline of her nightgown. She felt the deep, shuddering breath that passed through him, and the stirring of his body against her thighs. 'Get off me, woman,' he groaned, and shut his eyes again.

'You're lying on my arm.'

'Mm?' The heavy lids lifted and he stared at her.

'I can't move it,' Katrien explained, fighting the urge to lower her mouth the few inches that would bring her lips to his. He might be in pain, but he was reacting physically to her, and couldn't hide it. Would it be immoral to take advantage of his weakness? She supposed it would.

He didn't stir for several seconds, then he sighed and rolled sideways, freeing her arm, but the movement had brought them momentarily even closer, his body crowding hers, his arm about her preventing her from falling off the edge of the bed. For perhaps two seconds she held her breath, while the heat of his skin penetrated her thin gown, and her breasts were crushed to his hard chest. Then he rolled onto his back again, and lay with his arms at his sides, breathing deeply.

Carefully Katrien disentangled herself. 'Let me see your ankle.'

'Just go away, Katrien!'

'I can't. You're in pain and I can help.'

'Oh, hell!' he said finally, flinging an arm across his eyes. 'Then do me one favour, will you? Go and put on some clothes first!'

She did, and came back exuding efficiency and brisk concern in the face of his tight-lipped stoicism. The ankle had swelled badly, and he reluctantly let Katrien take him to her GP and have it checked. He was told he'd have to rest it for a couple of days and then be cautious about using it.

'I can't go to Sydney,' she said.

'You will damn well go,' he insisted. 'I'll be all right.'

'I can't—'

'I've twisted my bloody ankle!' he shouted at her. 'That's no reason for you to jeopardise your career. Don't be so damned silly!'

She opened her mouth to shout back at him, smarting at the insult. But of course he was right. 'I'll ask Miranda to look in on you,' she said. 'Otherwise I'll be worried all day.'

His mouth straightened ominously. Then he said grittily, 'All right. If it makes you feel better.'

She left before six and when she arrived back from the trip late that night she caught him with his leg up on the sofa, lying back against the cushions with his eyes closed. Half a dozen tapes were scattered randomly on the coffee table. For a moment she wondered if he'd been waiting up for her.

He lifted his head when she came in, and gave a smile that lit his face before he schooled it to a polite, expressionless mask. 'How was the audition?' he asked.

'All right, I think.' She put down the flight bag she carried, leaving it on the floor. 'How was your day?'

He shrugged. Then, with a disgusted little laugh, he said, 'I've been fooling myself—' he indicated the scattered tapes '—thinking I can shape these ramblings into a book.'

'You haven't even had them typed up yet. May I listen to them?' She hadn't dared ask before.

'You must be tired.'

'It'll help me unwind.'

The first one began with a description of the preparation for the fatal Himalayan expedition, much of it technical. Then he detailed the journey to Nepal, and setting up a base camp at the foot of the target mountain. The narrative picked up there, interspersed with brief memories of other climbs and descriptions of local people and fellow climbers.

Zachary got up and hobbled to the window. 'Turn it off,' he said. 'No publisher in his right mind would be interested.'

'You need a ghost writer,' she suggested.

'Isn't that cheating?'

'Not if the writer is mentioned as a co-author.' A thought that had been half forming in her mind came to her lips. 'I'd like to give it a go.'

He looked impatient, rather than grateful. 'I am not taking any more favours from you, Katrien.'

'How about doing me one, then? Modelling isn't a long-term career. I have maybe five, at the most ten years left. Meantime I hope to build my name as a writer. Having my name on the cover of a book would be good exposure for Kate Winston.'

It took a bit more persuasion, but eventually he said, 'I'll pay you for it, of course.'

She knew he wanted Wendy to benefit from the book, but maybe this wasn't the time to say she was happy to work without payment. 'Let me sort out two or three chapters and then we'll talk to the publisher. We can discuss the details then if they're interested.'

She worked on the tapes steadily for the next two days, transcribing into her computer, and editing. It gave her something to concentrate on besides Zachary's presence. He filled the time reading, listening to music on her stereo, or watching television. If anything, since his fall he'd been more determined than ever to avoid touching her. But the tension crackled between them so palpably she could almost see it.

Finally she handed him a list of chapter numbers with notes under each. 'And this is a rough draft of the first few pages.'

While he was reading, she microwaved some chicken pieces, sliced bread into a basket, and made a salad.

He came into the kitchen as she placed the chicken on the table. 'This is brilliant,' he said almost grudgingly. Had he hoped she would botch the job?

'It's very rough, but I hope you can see how I want it to shape up. There are some technical bits I'll have to ask you to explain, and a few gaps.'

'Like what?'

Katrien hesitated. 'There's nothing on the tape about how...how Ben Storey died.'

His face went hard. 'That isn't for public consumption.'

'I understand your feelings, but a publisher—'

'You don't understand a thing! I won't add to Wendy's grief by describing her husband's last moments for every stranger who buys the book.'

'Why don't you ask her how she feels about it?'

'How would *you* feel?' he shot at her.

'It hasn't happened to me—'

'And it never will!' he said forcefully.

'But shouldn't the decision be hers?'

'I don't want to burden her with it, make her feel as if she has to agree.'

'I thought you two knew each other better than that.'

He scowled. 'I'll think about it.'

She was into the second chapter later that day when Zachary made her a cup of coffee and put it down on the table beside her.

'Thank you,' she said absently, picking it up. Then she looked at his hands. 'Zachary, that's great!'

Of course she was glad—she wanted him to get back to normal. But although he'd been scrupulously courteous and before he had injured his ankle again he had shown signs of thawing into something resembling friendship a couple of times, ever since that day when he had betrayed his involuntary physical reaction to her he had erected a mental wall between them and was firmly keeping her on the other side of it.

Wendy phoned again. Hearing the warmth in his greeting, Katrien reflected wistfully that he never used that note of affection with her.

'Yes,' he was saying, 'I'm being looked after very well. But I can't impose on Katrien's hospitality for much longer.'

About to leave the room, she turned to protest. 'You're not...'

'Yes, put them on,' he said, and she guessed the girls were clamouring to talk to him. 'Hi, honey. Yes, it's Uncle Zach. Sure I'll come and see you as soon as I can. Yes, it's a promise... Hello, little one. Sorry—I guess you *are* a big girl.' He smiled tenderly, and Katrien wished stupidly that just once he would smile like that at her. 'Your birthday? Maybe. I'll try to make it. No, your daddy won't be with me, sweetheart. Not this time.' The smile faded and his eyes went bleak.

Katrien felt tears burning in her own eyes. It must be difficult for a nearly-three-year-old to comprehend that her father had died. Particularly a father who had been in the habit of being away from home for weeks or months at a time.

Zachary spoke briefly again to Wendy, and then replaced the receiver. 'The girls miss their father.'

'Wendy too.' And you, Katrien thought.

'Yes. She and Ben—they had something special.'

'Then why did he—?' Katrien broke off. Zachary wouldn't thank her for criticising his dead friend.

'Wendy understood,' Zachary said.

'His children don't!'

A shadow fell across Zachary's face. 'No. You're right.' There was a harsh note in his voice. 'Yasmin wants me to come to her birthday party.'

Cold dread descended on her. 'When?'

'Next Saturday.' He looked down at his hands and flexed them. 'I have to be there. For Ben's sake. Since he's gone, I guess I'm the next best thing.'

So little time. Katrien stood dumbly. There was nothing she could do to hold him. And anyway, she couldn't be so selfish. 'I suppose,' she said reluctantly, 'you do have to be there.' She asked painfully, 'Will you come back?'

'Here?' He looked about the room, then back at her. 'Not a good idea.'

Of course he didn't think so. He'd reluctantly remained after the debacle of that first evening, resenting his dependence and expending all the energy he could muster on getting himself fit enough to leave again as soon as possible.

'What about the book?' she asked him.

'You've got the tapes. You don't need me any more, do you?'

Katrien hesitated. 'The publisher you mentioned. He's in Auckland, isn't he? Maybe you should contact him before you go.' Most publishing houses, she knew, were turning away writers in droves, but this one had approached Zachary. She supposed Zachary's celebrity status made a difference.

'I want to thank you,' Zachary told her the day before he was due to leave for Christchurch. 'I know I've seemed ungrateful.'

'I've done nothing I didn't want to.'

'Even giving Callum back his ring?'

'Our engagement was a mistake. I'm sorry I hurt him, but not sorry we realised that before it was too late.'

He looked at her in silence for a moment, then said rather abruptly, 'Would you let me take you out to dinner tonight? By way of a thank-you?'

Thank you and goodbye, he meant. She swallowed around a lump in her throat. 'That would be nice.'

Zachary booked a table for them at one of Auckland's top restaurants. He went out that afternoon in a taxi, and came home with a large plastic carrier bag. 'I didn't pack evening clothes when I went to Ruapehu,' he explained. 'Most of my stuff is at Ben's—Wendy's place in Christchurch.'

He'd told her he didn't have a place of his own, and between expeditions he rented short-term accommodation, or sometimes stayed with or house-sat for friends.

Tonight Katrien pulled out all the stops. She wore a simply cut, fitted long-sleeved sheath of burgundy lace that framed her shoulders, dipped slightly between her breasts, and showed off her narrow waist and curved hips. Her long, slim legs were flattered by high-heeled burgundy shoes. She piled her hair up in a deceptively casual look and fastened it with a single artificial white rose on a clip, and her make-up was discreet but flawless, her lips coloured a luscious pink. If Zachary was determined to walk out of her life she had no intention of making it easy for him.

When she picked up her small evening purse and a light wrap and entered the sitting room where he waited for her, she saw the stunned look in his eyes as he rose from his seat on the sofa, and gave him a smile of slow triumph. At the very least he was going to find it hard to forget her.

'You look—' His voice was low and gritty, and he stopped to clear his throat. 'Fantastic.'

'Thank you.' He looked fantastic himself in a dinner

jacket, and he'd got his hair cut, shorter than she'd ever seen it but sleekly styled. 'You too,' she told him.

His smile held a hint of reserve. He was still keeping that barrier between them. He might admire her, even desire her, but, although he'd said he understood why she'd deceived him about their supposed engagement, he hadn't forgiven her.

There was a discreet toot from outside, and he said, 'That'll be our taxi.'

This time he opened the front door for her, and as they walked to the cab she saw with a mixture of delight and sadness that he was hardly relying on his crutch at all.

In the restaurant he ordered sparkling wine, saying, 'We're celebrating, aren't we?'

'Yes.' She smiled. You may be celebrating; I'm dying inside.

The waiter came back and poured the wine with a flourish. Zachary caught Katrien's eye and they exchanged a look of covert amusement as the man departed.

'To your complete recovery,' she said lightly, lifting her glass to him.

'Thank you. And to your kind heart.' His mouth twisted ironically.

Katrien shook her head. 'That has nothing to do with it,' she said. 'Do you really believe I was sorry for you? Is that why you're so…angry?'

'Angry?'

'You are,' she insisted. 'Underneath.'

'Angry,' he repeated thoughtfully. 'I was, when I discovered you'd lied about our engagement.'

'I handled it badly,' she confessed. 'I meant to talk to Callum and tell him that you were with me. And then…break it to you that there'd been…a mistake.'

'Did you? Mean to break it to me?' He was looking

at his champagne glass, gently shifting it on the table-cloth.

Her eyes widened in dismay. 'Of course I did! You don't think I'd have gone on letting you believe...'

He looked up at her, his eyes filled with glittering curiosity. 'I wondered.'

The waiter brought their soup, and Zachary picked up his spoon.

'It may surprise you,' Katrien said frigidly, when the man had gone, 'but I was not exactly desperate for a husband. I had Callum, and as a matter of fact there's never been a shortage of offers.'

Zachary swallowed a spoonful of soup, put a napkin to his mouth, and laughed. 'That's put me in my place.'

'And furthermore,' she said relentlessly, refusing to be inveigled into laughing with him, 'when you asked me to come to your friends' lodge, I refused. Or don't you remember that?'

He sobered in an instant, and his eyes turned dark and probing. 'I remember very well. I also remember that you kissed me goodnight with some...enthusiasm.'

Katrien stirred her soup diligently. 'It was only a kiss.'

'It did seem to me to be more than mere gratitude.'

She looked up at him, meeting his eyes frankly. 'You know that I was...attracted to you. But I was still engaged to Callum.'

The waiter approached their table. 'Is your soup all right, madam?'

'Yes,' she said. She hadn't tasted it. 'Thank you.'

The soup was getting cold. She began slowly spooning it up. Zachary didn't seem in any hurry to take advantage of the opening she'd given him. He was probably wondering how to tactfully extricate himself.

'I shouldn't have let you take me home,' Zachary said abruptly. 'I stuffed up your life, didn't I?'

'No!' She put down her spoon and pushed away the

unfinished soup. 'I wanted you there. I wanted to…look after you. Nobody forced me into it.'

'I just made it difficult for you not to offer.' He sounded disgusted with himself. 'I should have gone to Wendy then. Or anyone else.'

'Has it been that bad?' She looked at him and gave him a tentative smile. She could hardly be unaware that he'd hated being dependent on her, but then he'd have hated being dependent on anyone. And there had been moments—rare ones, admittedly—when he'd let the defences he'd built slip and they'd enjoyed something almost like friendship.

'It has,' he said, 'been sheer torture.'

Katrien flinched. She couldn't help it.

He saw it, of course, and swiftly closed his eyes, then opened them again. 'Oh, hell! Katrien—I didn't mean I don't appreciate what you've done…'

'Then what did you mean?' she challenged him. She knew he'd been attracted to her initially. And at Ruapehu he had been well aware she felt the same about him, despite her commitment to Callum. He'd said he understood that her deception hadn't been deliberate. So why was he still punishing her for it? Because that was what it felt like.

'All right,' he said at last. 'If you want it spelled out— I mean that living in the same house with you, looking at you all day and having you do every damned little thing for me, has been sending me quietly crazy.'

'Why?' Her voice was scarcely above a whisper. But she was going to make him spell out his feelings whether he wanted to or not.

'You know damned well why,' he told her roughly. 'Because I want you so much I can hardly see straight!'

CHAPTER NINE

KATRIEN tried to smile, her lips trembling. 'You could have fooled me,' she told him. 'Sometimes I thought you hated me.'

'Hate you?' Zachary shook his head. 'I...' He stopped there, and looked away from her.

She fought a sharp sense of disappointment. For an instant she'd hoped that he was going to say he loved her.

Their soup plates were taken away, and Katrien stretched out her hand and put it over one of Zachary's. 'There's nothing wrong with your hands now,' she said.

The one she held turned and grasped hers tightly. Zachary made a sound that was half groan, half laughter. 'Katrien...what are you saying?'

She smiled straight into his eyes. 'I'm saying that there's nothing to stop you touching me now. All you want.' She could hardly make herself plainer than that, she thought.

She was unprepared for the blaze that entered the green depths. 'Damn it, Katrien!' he said. 'Don't!' But his hand was gripping hers to the point of pain.

Her smile wavered. Had she made a fool of herself? 'What are you afraid of?' she asked him quietly. Because he'd just admitted that he wanted her, that she hadn't been wildly wrong about that.

'Afraid?' His shoulders went rigid, and he released her hand.

'This isn't a trap. I just want...'

'A one-night stand?' he said harshly. 'Would that satisfy you, Katrien?'

She recoiled from him, feeling the muscles of her face go rigid with hurt. She'd cheapened herself for nothing, practically offering herself to him on a plate. She had tried not to think beyond tonight, but his bluntness forced her to face her own inner motives.

Of course she wouldn't be satisfied. Casual sex went against all her most cherished principles. Deep down, she'd hoped that once they had shared the greatest intimacy possible between two adult human beings, he would be hers for ever. That he wouldn't be able to leave her.

'You should have stuck with Callum,' he said bleakly. 'I can't offer you what he did.'

Marriage. A lifetime of security.

Carefully, she said, 'I haven't asked you for that, have I? What are you trying to do, Zachary—save me from myself? As though I were a child who has to be kept away from the fire because she might get hurt? I resent that. I'm a grown woman, I know exactly what I want, and I'm prepared to take whatever consequences might arise. So don't make my decisions for me, okay? Of course, whatever you want to do—' she shrugged with all the pseudo-nonchalance she could muster '—is up to you.'

She saw the flush that marked his cheekbones, and his eyes narrowed. He seemed to be struggling inwardly with himself.

Finally he spoke, his voice low and gritty. 'You know what I want to do. I've wanted to make love to you since I first set eyes on you at that dinner, and I could hardly remember the words of my speech for looking at you. When you looked back at me I lost it altogether. As soon as I realised you'd disappeared without speaking to me

I raced out to try and stop you leaving—and you introduced me to your fiancé.'

Katrien stared at him, mesmerised by the dark passion in his voice.

'The day you turned up at Ruapehu I thought it was fate,' he said. 'Or that somehow you'd followed me. I hoped you had. But then I saw you were still wearing your engagement ring.'

He stared down at her naked hands, and she said, 'I'm not wearing it any more.'

'No.' He took her fingers again in his. As if the words were wrung from him, he said, 'I hope you won't regret this.'

Their main course was put before them, but Katrien could scarcely eat hers. They finished the champagne and Zachary ordered another bottle, his eyes gleaming as he silently toasted her. And by mutual consent they skipped dessert, going straight to coffee and liqueurs.

Before they left the restaurant Katrien visited the ladies' room and checked her appearance in the mirror. Her cheeks were faintly flushed, and her eyes appeared languorous and sexy and expectant. She flushed more deeply, looking at herself, and hurried out to meet Zachary coming out of the door on the opposite side of the carpeted lobby. In the taxi he held her hand, his thumb stroking the back of it, and as soon as they got inside the front door of the flat he dropped his crutch, pulled her into his arms and began kissing her.

Katrien wound her arms about his neck and kissed him back, her mouth parting for him, inviting him, her body pressed against his, curving to its hard masculine contours.

She led him through the darkness to her bedroom, and began slowly to undo the knot of his tie and unbutton his shirt. He must have fastened it himself when he was dressing, and she quelled a selfish pang of regret that he no longer needed her.

When she had parted all the buttons she slipped a hand inside the shirt, her fingers roving over the warm skin, and he clasped her head between his hands and kissed her again.

Her palm measured the thudding of his heart. She pushed his shirt aside, stepping out of her shoes, and when his mouth briefly left hers, she whispered, 'Your ankle must be hurting. You should lie down.'

'We both should,' he murmured, and lowered her with him down onto the bed.

She removed herself from his arms to kneel by his feet, taking off his shoes and socks. She lifted his injured ankle and gently massaged it, holding it on her thighs. 'Better?' she asked him.

'Infinitely. Why didn't they give you a job in the physio department at the hospital?'

She laughed softly and moved her hand further up his leg. Zachary leaned forward and caught her wrist and drew her to him until she was lying along the length of his body. One hand held her head as he kissed her, the other slid down the long zip at the back of her dress.

Between kisses and caresses they undressed each other and stripped off the bedcover and slipped between the sheets.

'I knew it would be like this,' he whispered. 'Like my dreams. All those dreams I had when I was lying out in the snow, and later, in the hospital.'

'You dreamed of me when you were unconscious?'

'Nothing else. And every night since. You—lying in my arms like this, kissing me like this...'

'Touch me,' she whispered back to him. 'Touch me in all the ways you dreamed about...I've dreamed about. I want your hands on me again...'

'Again?'

Hazily she was aware that his wonderful, sensitive, roving hands had stilled. She took one of them in hers, holding it to her breast. 'Please. Like you do always. Please, I've missed you, it's seemed so long. This time—'

'Damn it, Katrien!' Suddenly he had left her, flinging himself away from her to twist round and switch on the bedside light, dazzling her. Furiously he turned back to her, taking her by the shoulders as if he'd like to shake her. 'I'm not Callum!'

Disoriented, she said blankly, 'I know you're not!'

Zachary's eyes blazed into hers, then they narrowed, and she knew a shiver of fear. 'So who is the wonderful lover whose touch you've missed so much?'

Remembering what she'd said in the heat of passion, she blushed all over. 'You.'

If anything, he looked more furious than ever. There was a dreadfully controlled stillness about him. 'We have never made love before, and you know it.'

She got up on her knees to put her hands on his chest, moving them to his shoulders. 'But we have,' she told him softly. 'Often, in my dreams. Ever since I was fourteen.'

For a brief moment his expression had lightened, but at her final words he frowned again. 'What?'

'It might not have been important to you,' she said. 'But I never forgot you. I couldn't. You've always been in my dreams. Sometimes it's frightening, like it was when you grabbed me and got me onto the surfboard. I didn't realise what was happening—I'd blacked out in the water, and the next thing I knew someone's mouth was on mine, but I didn't realise what he was doing, and when I began to breathe on my own and started to fight, he seemed to be manhandling me and it felt…rough.

Later of course I knew that you'd had no time to be gentle. You seemed so angry, and it wasn't until afterwards that I remembered the words—all I could hear at the time was the tone. You were telling me not to die, that I was damn well not going to die.'

She smiled into his narrowed, fixed eyes. 'And later it was comforting. Encouraging. You kept saying I was going to be all right, promising you would get me back to the beach. By that time I was shaking and clinging to you and begging you not to let go.'

'You were terrified.' Zachary's eyes darkened between their lowered lids.

'Hysterical,' Katrien admitted shamefacedly. 'Out of my mind with fear.'

His eyes flickered.

'And then…' she recalled '…then you kissed me.'

The brief pressure of his mouth had been warm and compelling, and an astonished sweetness had flooded her chilled, shivering body and jolted her into an awareness of something other than stark, frenzied fear. 'No one had ever kissed me like that.'

'Like what?' he said. And then added forcefully, 'It wasn't meant to be sexual! It was instinctive, to reassure you that you'd be okay if you'd just stop panicking and do what I said. Seduction was the last thing on my mind!'

'I know that. You had to calm me down—I was putting us both in danger, clinging onto you for dear life so you couldn't swim or manoeuvre the board. We might have both drowned if you hadn't done something drastic.'

'Slapping you might have been better,' he muttered. 'If I'd been able to get a hand free—'

But he hadn't dared to risk either letting go of her or losing the surfboard. 'The kiss worked,' she reminded him. 'It stopped me being so silly. And then you just said, "Trust me." And I did.'

'Didn't your mother ever tell you not to trust a man who said that?' He spoke wryly.

Katrien gave a small laugh. 'Just as well I didn't listen. Otherwise I would have died that day.'

'Katrien—'

'So now you know,' she said. 'You've been my dream lover for years. The man all other men were measured by. The man who came to me in the night and…made love to me. Never fully. I always woke before…before the end. But you kissed me and touched me and made me long for more. And as I grew older the dreams became more and more…explicit. But not enough. I always woke…disappointed.'

By the time she met Callum she'd convinced herself her dream man was just that—a fantasy figure that had evolved from a time when her awakening sexuality had become inextricably linked with the most traumatic experience she had ever had. And that no one could ever live up to the unreal figure she had created in her mind.

'Tonight,' she said, 'all my dreams are coming true at last.' She stroked his cheek. 'My dream man has a face now—'

'What do you mean?' Zachary looked both shaken and wary.

'I never could see what he looked like until I met you—met you again. The night of the charity dinner, for the first time I could see his face—your face. I know now who you are.' At his appalled expression, she laughed tenderly. 'I know you hate being called a hero, but you are. My brave, strong, wonderful dream-man hero.'

She leaned forward to kiss him, and was stunned when

Zachary flung her back on the pillows and escaped the tangled covers to stand up.

'No!' His face was white. 'God almighty, Katrien, why do you have to complicate things? I'm not your hero. I'm nobody's bloody *hero!*' He stooped to pick up his clothes, gathering them all together untidily.

'What are you doing? Zachary, come back—'

He shook his head, his mouth tight. 'You don't want a real man, you want a dream, an imaginary white knight.' His look at her was a searing accusation.

Instinctively she pulled the covers up over her breasts. 'I want *you*,' she told him unsteadily. 'I know you're real—'

'No, you don't. You don't know what reality is. You've been living in some dreamworld of adolescent hero-worship. I can't live up to this image you've created for me, Katrien. I'm not the man you've been dreaming about. I never was.'

He left her, and she heard the door of his room slam as he entered it. She sank down under the covers, her body getting colder and colder, until she started to shiver.

It was a long time before she slept, and when she woke in the morning to hear Zachary moving about already, she buried her head in the pillow, passionately wishing she didn't have to face him.

The taxi driver carried Zachary's luggage to the car. Katrien knew that Zachary would have hated her to offer, so she'd asked the man to do it, explaining that his passenger had been in an accident.

Zachary followed the man, leaning on his crutch, and paused in the hallway to look down at Katrien where she stood near the door. 'Thank you for everything,' he said formally. 'You've been very generous with your time and...attentions. I won't be telling anyone except Wendy that we were never really engaged.'

'Thank you.' It hardly mattered, really, Katrien thought dully. She hesitated briefly. But this might be her only, last chance. She stepped forward, slipped her arms about his neck, and kissed him.

She felt him stiffen, and his mouth for an instant was unresponsive. She moved her lips over his, willing him to respond, and when he did it was devastating. His mouth drove against hers, and he pushed her back, his hard body trapping her, one hand and forearm slamming the wall. The kiss went on and on, deeper and deeper, until she was dizzy and the hot blood pounded in her head.

'Need help on the steps, mate?' A voice penetrated the hot haze of desire, and gradually, unhurriedly, Zachary's mouth left hers.

'No. Be with you in a minute,' he said, not taking his eyes away from Katrien's face. Dimly she saw the driver put his head around the half-open door, then hastily retreat.

For a moment longer Zachary didn't move. Then he dropped his arm abruptly and stepped away from her, steadying himself with the crutch.

His eyes looked dark and angry. He seemed to have difficulty dragging his gaze away from her. Then he turned and without another word limped out the door and carefully down the steps.

She watched him all the way to where the taxi stood waiting to take him to the airport, and he didn't look back once.

Perhaps it was because she didn't care that she was chosen to be the Snowfire girl. If she'd been asked to adopt a cheerful, bubbly persona she would have found it almost impossible, but it wasn't difficult to convey the required air of hidden fires under an icy cool exterior. That was how she felt most of the time, as though a film of ice had descended over a smouldering fire of need and passion mingled with hurt fury.

'You've fallen on your feet,' Hattie enthused. 'You're very lucky.'

Katrien didn't feel lucky; she felt as if she were burning slowly to death from the inside.

A letter came for Zachary, with the publisher's logo on the envelope. Katrien phoned Wendy Storey's number, her palm slippery on the receiver.

Wendy's light, pleasant voice floated down the line. 'It's nice to hear from you,' she said. 'How are you?'

'I'm fine,' Katrien lied. 'How is Zachary doing?'

'Well…he's walking a lot, exercising the ankle, and going to the gym regularly. He seems to be doing his best to exhaust himself.'

Wendy sounded worried. Katrien chewed on her lower lip. 'I guess he wants to climb again,' she said half-bitterly.

'I don't suppose you'd care to try and talk some sense into him?' Wendy asked.

'If he won't listen to you, he certainly won't listen to me,' Katrien told her.

Wendy lowered her voice. 'What happened between you two? Zachary said it was all a mistake, that the media got things twisted.'

'Yes. I'm sorry if you had the wrong impression, but we were never more than friends.'

'Oh?' Wendy was obviously doubtful. 'Well, you made a great job of pulling him through this. I'm glad you were around.'

A child in the background said something, and Wendy

answered, the sound muffled by a hand over the receiver. 'Zachary's coming,' she said. 'Bye, Katrien, take care.'

'Katrien?' He seemed so near, so vital.

'Zachary.' She took a quick, steadying breath. 'There's a publisher's letter. Shall I send it on to you?'

'Open it,' he said.

She read it out to him. The editor was very interested in the story, and happy with what Katrien had done. If Zachary was agreeable he'd like to discuss some minor points and talk about a contract.

'I'll phone him,' Zachary said, 'and suggest he talks to you, if that's okay. You're the writer, after all.' With sudden reserve, he added, 'That's if you're still willing.'

She'd been afraid he'd want to take the project out of her hands. 'I am,' she said firmly. 'Of course, I may need to consult with you sometimes.' She wouldn't, she promised herself, do so unless it was truly necessary. She wouldn't beg for crumbs.

Katrien put down the phone with an oddly empty feeling. So that's that, she said to herself. Zachary's managing just fine without you. And getting himself in a fit state to return to his first and only love—the mountains.

She ought to be glad for him. Instead she felt a flaring of the obscure anger that most of the time she kept deliberately tamped down.

The Snowfire photo shoots and commercials kept her working hard for several weeks, on both sides of the Tasman. Katrien was glad of being kept too busy to think most of the time, except about obeying the photographer's and director's instructions and making sure she delivered 'the look' that they wanted.

She put her laptop into her bag wherever she went, and when she had waiting time she would bring part of the transcript of Zachary's tapes to the screen and work on it. Shaping his words, she felt she knew him better with each day.

When she was lucky she slept well and without dreaming. But there were mornings when she woke with the memory of sea-green eyes burning into hers, and of unfulfilled passion that made her body warm and restless.

The Snowfire launch was accomplished with simultaneous releases in Australia and New Zealand—a blitz of TV and magazine publicity.

The company had used the image of Ruapehu, a white mountain exploding in fire, as the backdrop to their commercials. She became accustomed to her own face staring at her from billboards, and seeing herself on every TV channel.

The first TV ad began with the mountain in the background, and Katrien appeared first as a vague shape rising mistily out of a snow-covered landscape like a wraith, gradually turning into a woman in a shimmering, ethereal silver gown, her hands cradling one of the distinctive frosted hourglass Snowfire bottles with their elegant flame-shaped amber glass tops. Looking mysteriously into the camera, she held the bottle to her cheek, and then lowered it to slowly remove the stopper, releasing a cloud of white vapour that wreathed about her face and when it touched her hair burst into sudden flame, blowing back from her face in an artificial wind. Lifting her head, she slowly closed her eyes, feigning ecstasy, then opened them and straight to the camera whispered, 'Snow-fi-ire,' her reddened lips pouting into the first syllable, then drawing out the second, the echo of it dying away as her hair became a vertical flame and her image faded, merging into the elegant waisted shape of the Snowfire container.

She had actually been nowhere near snow. Her part

had been filmed in the studio, and computerised special effects had supplied the rest. The commercial had caused comment in the press, the makers of Snowfire were pleased with initial product recognition, and sales were promising.

More and more often Katrien saw people do a double-take when they passed her in the street. Callum sent her flowers with a congratulatory card, and followed with a phone call.

She thanked him warmly for the flowers, some part of her heart aching for what they had once shared, for the plans they had made together, and sorrowing for his loss and hers.

But it would be cruel to give him false hope. As tact-fully as possible she declined his suggestion of a meeting. When he hinted that he'd been seeing someone, she guessed this was a last-ditch attempt at reconciliation before he gave up on her and turned his attention to a new love. Or perhaps it was a salvaging of his pride. Either way she wished him well, and told him so, erasing every hint of sadness from her voice. She was sorry she'd hurt him, and that she hadn't been able to give him what he had needed and deserved. But if she couldn't have Zachary, she didn't want any other man.

She had sent more material to the publisher and after talking to him again she had to phone Zachary.

'He said it's promising,' she told him. 'He likes it.'

'Good.'

'But he doesn't want just another story of a failed expedition. I...told him it's more than that. It's about a friendship that was forged in the mountains, and ended there.'

The silence became ominous. 'I know what you want.'

'If you can't do it, or you feel it's not right, I'll try

to complete the book without it. But...I know it would
be a better book...'

'I'll talk to Wendy,' he promised grudgingly.

She was asked to take part in a twelve-hour midday-to-
midnight television fundraiser for a children's wing to
be built onto a hospital in Nepal. 'The Snowfire mar-
keting people think it would be good exposure,' her
agent told her. 'The organisers would like you to stay
through the whole twelve hours, helping the professional
presenter, but a lot of the guests will only make a brief
appearance.'

Wearing her silver 'Snowfire' gown, Katrien was the
telethon's star attraction. Twice she was asked to repeat
the now famous 'Snow-fi-ire' whisper on camera for the
benefit of viewers who pledged handsome sums for the
privilege of seeing her do so. When not at a microphone
alongside the male disc jockey who was the mainstay of
the show, she 'worked the floor', collecting money from
people who visited the studio.

Due on camera again towards the end of the show,
she spent fifteen minutes in the ladies' room freshening
up and she returned to the studio in time to hear the
presenter say, 'And of course you helped build part of
the hospital where the new children's wing is planned,
didn't you?'

The man beside him answered, 'There were several
New Zealanders involved, but the local people did most
of the work.'

Katrien walked forward and with a sense of inevitabil-
ity took the empty seat alongside the new guest. She
ought to have been prepared for this. It was only logical
that the organisers would have contacted people who had
connections with Nepal and the Himalayas.

People like Zachary Ballantine.

CHAPTER TEN

A SMATTERING of applause greeted Katrien's return. The presenter said, 'And it's great to have you with us, Zachary. You and Katrien know each other, of course.'

Only then did Zachary turn to her. He looked more relaxed than she felt, but she couldn't read his expression. He leaned over and gave her a quick, meaningless kiss on the cheek. Her skin had cooled when she'd seen him, but where his lips had touched her it suddenly burned.

She glanced at his hands and saw that they appeared quite normal, the fingers long and straight. Katrien suppressed an urge to put her own hands over them.

The presenter said breezily, 'And the Snowfire girl is back with us, along with famous climber Zachary Ballantine, survivor of the disastrous expedition to the Himalayas just about a year ago. Terrible tragedy, but we're glad you made it, Zach. And Katrien has been here since we started, of course, doing a great job with the punters. Not surprising, is it?' He smiled conspiratorially at Zach. 'Who could turn down a gorgeous girl like her?'

Katrien caught Zachary's eyes with hers and gave him a stiff, ironic smile. He could, and he had, but she couldn't say that to a nationwide audience. And she didn't suppose he would either.

Holding her gaze, he said, 'Katrien's very good at charity work.'

'Really?' The presenter's eyes gleamed behind his horn-rimmed glasses. 'Well, she's certainly doing a grand job here. Keep those pledges coming, folks. Think of all the little Nepalese kiddies who are going to benefit from what *you* can donate today. Zachary, you have a pile of pledges there—would you read some out for us?'

She wanted to close her eyes and listen to the dark honey voice, but instead she stared straight ahead, fiddled with the sheaf of papers before her, and when the studio light indicated she was on camera, fixed an interested smile on her face.

A troupe of children took the floor and performed an Indian dance, and a man with a talking parrot followed them. Although Katrien tried to ignore the presence of the man at her side, she was aware of every breath he took, every movement he made.

The presenter good-naturedly descended to the studio floor and did ten push-ups on request for a viewer who pledged a fifty-dollar donation.

Someone placed a pile of pledges in front of Katrien and she read out the names. One man promised a hundred dollars if the Snowfire girl would blow him a kiss on camera.

'I'm sure you've made his day,' the presenter said gaily when she had complied. 'Now, here's one—' He paused. 'The girls at Swatches Curtains pledge *three* hundred dollars! They voted Zachary Ballantine the sexiest mountain man around, and want the Snowfire girl to give him a nice big, passionate kiss on their behalf. So how about it, Katrien? I think I can guarantee Zachary won't object.' He waggled his puckish eyebrows.

Katrien's smile froze.

The audience was clapping happily. Zachary slowly turned to her. 'I'm all yours,' he murmured.

I wish you were, she thought.

She looked up slowly, lifted her mouth and pressed it to his. Feeling the firm, warm shape of his lips, she let hers linger longer than she'd meant to, and suddenly his hands were in her hair, and he'd taken over the kiss, his mouth moving sensually on hers.

Dimly she heard the cheers and whistles of the crowd. Her hands went to Zachary's shoulders, trying to remind him that they were on camera. Through his shirt she could feel the tensile strength of his muscles, the heat of his skin. She found herself holding him instead of pushing him away, wanting the kiss to go on for ever.

It couldn't, of course. At last Zachary drew away, and dazedly she removed her hands from his shoulders and clasped them hard in her lap.

'Well,' the presenter laughed. 'That certainly generated a bit of heat in the studio—from the Snowfire girl herself, and mountain man Zachary Ballantine. That was for the girls at Swatches. I hope you enjoyed it as much as our two guests seemed to.'

Soon afterwards Zachary was replaced by a well-known rugby player. Katrien should have felt relief, but somehow a lot of the excitement had gone out of the day. There were only a few hours to go to midnight and the end of the telethon, and some guests who had appeared earlier on the show were coming back for the finale. She busied herself by helping with the collecting, and when the grand total went up at last she joined in the applause and the celebratory dance around the studio.

There were people all over the floor, some dancing in a conga-type line, others hugging and congratulating one another. The disc jockey grabbed Katrien and hugged her too. 'You were great!' he told her. 'Simply marvellous.'

'You too.' Over the entire twelve hours, he'd made do with snatching short breaks here and there. 'You did a wonderful job.'

She caught a glimpse of Zachary standing in a doorway. As she watched, he turned and disappeared. 'Excuse me,' she said breathlessly, and sped towards the door, picking up her roomy bag on the way.

Outside the building a cab was whisking some people away. It was cool, and in her flimsy dress she shivered.

Zachary's voice said beside her, 'Are you going home wearing that?'

She turned. 'I…I hoped I'd get a taxi quickly.'

He was frowning. 'Don't you have a jacket?'

Fumbling for it in her bag, she said, 'I didn't think it would be so cold. It's supposed to be nearly summertime.'

She almost dropped the bag, pulling out her light woollen jacket. Zachary reached out and took both bag and jacket, put the bag down on the pavement, and held the jacket for her.

Katrien turned to slip her arms into the sleeves. 'Thank you.'

He picked up her bag. 'I have a car around the corner. I'll take you home.'

'You don't need to—'

Her arm was taken in a firm grip. 'Come on,' he said.

He put her in the car and swung the bag onto the back seat. When he slid in beside Katrien she said, 'It's very kind of you.'

'Don't talk rubbish. You know damn well I wouldn't have offered if I hadn't wanted to see you.'

He didn't seem very pleased about it. She deliberately steadied the wildly hopeful beating of her heart.

'I was going to contact you anyway,' Zachary said.

'What about?' she asked warily.

'That tape you asked for.'

'Yes?' she prompted cautiously.

'I have it for you.'

'You did it?'

'You asked me to, didn't you?'

She was tempted to remind him that he didn't have a history of doing things because she'd asked for them, but held her tongue.

He slowed for a set of traffic lights on the hill, then speeded up again. It had been raining, and the road reflected the lights of the city. 'It's good to see you can drive,' Katrien offered. 'You must be glad to have your independence back.'

He gave a strange little crack of laughter at that, and Katrien said anxiously, 'You are all right, aren't you?'

'Yes. The doctors have cleared me to climb again.'

Her chest felt hollow. 'I'm…glad for you.'

'Thank you.'

She was sure she hadn't imagined the sarcasm in the short, banal phrase. Turning to him, she said, 'What's the matter, then?'

Street lamps cast intermittent shadows on his face. He glanced at her, but in the gloom she couldn't see his expression. 'What could be the matter? My life is exactly the way I want it.'

She thought he sounded as though he was trying to convince himself.

His head swivelled briefly towards her. 'And you…? I guess this Snowfire thing is a step up in your career. I see your picture everywhere.'

'It's steady work, and well-paid.'

Zachary nodded. 'Seen Callum lately?'

'No. I think he has another lady.'

He flicked a glance at her. 'Do you mind?'

Katrien shook her head. As if he cared, anyway.

After a while he drew up outside her flat, switched off the engine and turned in his seat. They sat in silence for a moment. She stirred. 'It's late. Thank you for the ride.'

He leaned over, bringing a waft of his special, unique

male scent to her nostrils, and her heart skipped in anticipation, but he only opened the glove box in front of her and took out a small oblong object. The tape he'd spoken of. 'Here,' he said.

She took it and clutched it for a moment, then slipped it into the pocket of her jacket.

'I'll bring your bag.' Zachary pushed open his door.

He followed her up the path with her bag in his hand. Katrien rummaged in her purse for the key and turned to unlock the door and swing it open.

She reached to take the bag from Zachary just as he bent to place it on the floor. They collided softly, and the bag dropped.

'Sorry,' she said breathlessly.

His hand was on her arm, rucking up the sleeve of the woollen jacket, his breath feathering her forehead. She breathed in the scent of him, and was assailed by a wave of longing so strong that she trembled, and felt herself sway towards him.

'Katrien?' he whispered, and clasped her other arm.

Unable to respond, she let her head droop against his shoulder, just wanting to be close to him for a few precious moments before he left her again.

'Katrien!' His voice was low and unsteady. His hands hardened on her arms as if he would have pushed her away, but then he gave a harsh groan and she felt the hot, sweet shock of his mouth on her exposed nape.

It lasted only a second, before he lifted his head and without looking at her, his cheek moving against the faintly dewed skin of her temple, muttered, 'God damn it, Katrien—ask me in.'

Katrien momentarily closed her eyes—afraid to let him in, afraid to send him away. She lifted heavy eyelids and tried to see his face, her eyes fearful. She hadn't yet flipped the light switch, and behind him the security lamp outside the flat cast his face in shadow. She had a strange sense of *déjà vu*, and was suddenly very calm and sure of herself. 'Yes,' she said. 'Come in.'

She stepped back and he came after her, his hands still gripping her shoulders, shoving the door shut behind him with his body. He gathered her to him as if he couldn't wait any longer, and as his lips closed over hers his hands slid the jacket away, following the fabric down her arms until he grasped her wrists in his, and held them while they stood body to body and their mouths clung, explored, discovered each other.

Then he stopped kissing her and reversed their positions, drawing her down the hallway after him as he backed towards her bedroom, his arms still loosely imprisoning her.

'This is not supposed to happen,' Zachary muttered, but he wasn't letting her go, and she hushed him with her fingers, then replaced them with her mouth.

'I've dreamed of you,' he said when they surfaced briefly, 'in that dress.' He held her away from him, watching how the fine, soft fabric shimmered in the darkness, hugging the contours of her body. He gave a low laugh. 'Half the men in the country must dream of you.' He leaned down to kiss her again, savoured her response and then took his mouth away. 'You've been driving me crazy. Everywhere I looked I saw your face—magazines, newspapers, television, billboards. You've haunted me.' They had reached the doorway of her bedroom and he took her fully into his arms again. 'Snowfire girl.'

The air was cool, but she was on fire. His mouth captivated hers, her skin giving off little invisible sparks where his hands touched her. The flimsy silver dress fell to the floor, and she was swept up in his arms and the shoes dropped from her feet. Cool sheets met her heated skin, and then she was warmed again by his hands, his body, his tender, passionate loving.

She felt weightless, floating on a sea of pleasure that was endless and infinite. His hands were magical, his mouth a miracle all on its own, inducing from her responses she had never known were possible, even better than her dreams.

He told her how beautiful she was, how desirable, and described to her how she made him feel when she touched him ever more boldly, when she kissed him on his mouth, his shoulder, the palm of his hand, and in even more intimate places.

He switched on the bedside light and stilled her small protest with a kiss, and lay beside her, stroking her naked body from head to toe with a single, feather-light, teasing finger, watching her feverish reaction with narrowed, glittering eyes. When he pulled her close again she punished him with tiny, nibbling bites on his shoulder, and he laughed and gently bit her earlobe in retaliation.

After turning aside for a moment, he spread her hair against the whiteness of the pillow, and touched her kiss-swollen lips with his thumb, and smiled at her, his eyes heavy-lidded but brilliant with passion. Then his hand swept down her body and urged her thighs apart, and he eased himself over her.

Katrien's breathing quickened, her eyelids flickering in delicious trepidation. Her hands slid about his shoulders, and she closed her eyes.

'Katrien?'

She opened her eyes again, looking up at the dark, flushed face above her. 'Come to me,' she whispered, 'Zachary.'

His face changed, taut and naked with desire. 'Yes,' he said, his voice deep, rasping. And she felt him sheathe himself within her, hot and heavy and hard.

She gasped, and went rigid, and his mouth came down, possessing her mouth as she possessed his body, taking her to a new plane of pleasure, sweeping her into the lovely, whirling maelstrom with him.

'Too fast for you?' he asked her a little later, tenderly arranging her tangled hair once more against the pillow.

He was propped on one elbow, and she loved the worried frown between his brows. Languidly she shook her head. 'Perfect.'

'Thank you, my lady.' He bent and kissed her softly.

She wished she was his lady. And he her man. But in all the romantic, passionate things he'd said to her, he'd made no promises.

She'd gone into this willingly, knowing that he wanted no emotional ties, no commitments. Pointless lamenting the fact. One day perhaps she would regret what she had done, but just now it was enough to have him here in her arms, in her bed.

'That,' he said, with a hint of unease, 'wasn't gratitude, was it?'

Katrien smiled lethargically. Suddenly she felt very, very tired. 'Did it feel like gratitude?' It was love, she thought. But even now he didn't want to hear that.

'It felt like heaven.' He rolled over and for a heart-stopping moment she was afraid he was going to get dressed and leave. But he only switched off the light. 'Is it all right if I stay?' he asked her, his voice deep and almost humble.

'It's all right,' she assured him, vastly relieved. 'Very all right.'

'Come here.' He found her in the darkness and gathered her into his arms.

She woke to find the sheets tumbled and Zachary gone. Apprehensive, she got out of the bed and pulled on a robe.

He was in the kitchen. 'I made coffee,' he said. 'I was going to bring you some in bed.'

'Thanks.' She searched his face, finding it perfectly neutral. 'I think I'll have a shower first.'

She showered quickly and pulled on undies, then the robe again before brushing her hair, leaving it loose. Her jacket still lay in a heap in the hall. She picked it up and went into the kitchen.

Zachary was fully dressed in the casual but respectable clothes he'd had on yesterday. He sat at the table with a cup in front of him, but when she appeared again he got up and poured one for her.

Katrien sat down opposite him and hung the jacket on the back of her chair. It swung against the wood and made a small clunking sound. She fished in the pocket and took out the tape Zachary had given her, placing it on the table between them.

'Play it after I'm gone,' he said.

'Gone?' Katrien looked up sharply, the blood leaving her cheeks.

'I stayed to take part in the telethon, but tomorrow—' he glanced at his watch '—today—I'm flying out to Katmandu. I just have to stop at my hotel and pick up some gear.'

'You're leaving...' Not just her, he was leaving the country. She should have known.

He was silent for a moment, apparently nonplussed. 'Last night—' He stopped and cleared his throat. 'It should never have happened. I'm sorry...the timing was lousy, but surely you heard me speak about this trip at the telethon.'

Katrien shook her head. 'You were talking about the hospital in Nepal.'

He looked oddly embarrassed, even worried. His voice was strange too. 'You didn't hear what we were discussing before that?'

'I was out of the studio for about fifteen minutes.' Her heart hammered in her chest. She knew. Of course she knew. 'You're going climbing there again,' she said, her voice flat, colourless.

She had a feeling she'd shocked him in some way. 'Yes. We kept it pretty much under wraps until now, because the peak's still unclimbed and we don't want someone stealing a march on us, but now it's all out in the open, and…I talked about it for quite a while at the telethon.'

Terror squeezed her heart. He was going back to the Himalayas; he could become trapped on some remote, treacherous peak and die there like Ben Storey. How could she bear it?

I love him. She cried it out silently in the innermost depths of her soul. I always have, always will.

But Zachary didn't want her love. He didn't want the love of any woman anchoring him to the earth, keeping him away from the clouds that misted his beloved mountains. The last words he wanted to hear from her were 'I love you'.

'It was Ben's dying wish,' Zachary said. 'He knew he wasn't going to make it after all, but he wanted me to do it, climb the bloody thing and get to the top for him.'

Katrien felt the blood buzzing in her ears. Zachary planned to go back to that killer mountain? 'And you're going to do it.'

'Yes,' he said. 'This time I'm going all the way. For Ben.'

Or die trying, Katrien supposed. She sat perfectly still, red spots swimming before her eyes. She was so angry she couldn't speak.

'I thought you'd heard.'

'If you get frostbite again—you know it gets worse each time!'

'I know.'

'You could lose a limb. You could die.'

'I could.' He sounded quite unemotional. 'The hazards are always there. It isn't any different from all the other climbs I've done.'

It *is* different! she thought fiercely. I didn't know you then—didn't love you—didn't have any idea what it was like to live in dread for someone else's life.

'I have to do it, Katrien.'

'For Ben.' She clenched her teeth. 'What about Wendy? She said she couldn't bear to lose you as well as her husband. What about those little girls? Aren't you trying to be some kind of surrogate daddy to them?'

She glanced at him, and saw his jaw go tight and stubborn. He didn't meet her eyes.

'Wendy—' he started.

'Don't tell me,' Katrien said bitterly. 'Wendy understands.' Wendy would have been a perfect wife for him, perhaps still would be. They had so much in common, and now that Ben was gone— She wondered bitterly if Ben Storey had bequeathed his wife to his best friend and climbing companion, along with the damned mountain he'd been so keen to conquer.

'Katrien—'

She pushed away the hand Zachary tried to lay on hers. 'Well, I don't!' she said wildly. 'I *can't* understand this mad compulsion to throw away your life and everything that—' That we might have had. The words choked her and she couldn't go on. If she said any more she'd end up screaming at him like some shrew. And she didn't have the right.

He had never pretended, never suggested that she

meant anything to him except a convenient nursemaid when he'd needed one—and even *that* he'd resented— and a woman he'd briefly wanted to bed. It was her own stupid fault that she'd fallen in love with him and let him make love to her without any intention of giving her anything more than the delights of his hard, beautiful male body. His mind, his heart belonged to the mountains.

They sat in tense silence for a few moments, then Zachary got up slowly and pushed his chair in. 'I'm sorry. I should never have come here. Last night was a huge mistake—a huge, selfish mistake on my part.'

Because he didn't love her and he knew damned well that she loved him. She wanted to make him acknowledge it; she wanted to beg him to stay, to let her love him for the rest of their lives.

That was the last thing he wished to hear, and it would only sear him with guilt. He might want her, but he didn't want her love. He had never asked for it, and she had no right to burden him with it.

'Listen to the tape,' he said. 'You needn't see me out.'

She sat there like a sculpture in ice and let him go, her heart crumbling into little pieces, her mouth dry, her throat locked. What good would it do to go after him, hang on his sleeve, cry? He wasn't going to be turned aside from his chosen way of life for anyone. Certainly not for her.

It was days before she could bring herself to play the tape. There was a short item in the newspaper about the departure of the new Himalayan expedition, with a brief reprise of the loss of the well-known mountaineer Ben Storey on a troubled expedition almost a year ago. Katrien folded the paper, picked up the tape and turned it over in her fingers.

Every other part of the book had been written and rewritten, spell-checked and polished, and the publisher was waiting for the finished product. She had to do this. She went and fetched the cassette player.

The sound of Zachary's voice coming from the machine sent an involuntary warmth down her spine. He spoke at first hesitantly, with frequent pauses, and then a woman's voice quietly prompted him. Wendy. Putting questions so calmly, murmuring comments as Zachary described to her how he and Ben had left the other members of the party in a bid to get to the top before nightfall, how they'd been slowed by an ice face, and how Ben had fallen, been injured despite Zachary's efforts to hold him, to halt his fall with the rope. 'Both his legs were broken, but I couldn't carry him in that terrain. I splinted them as best I could, and he couldn't walk on them, but he crawled back down through the snow until he was too exhausted to go any further.'

Zachary hesitated there until Wendy prompted him again, and then he took up the appalling story, describing Ben Storey's courageous efforts to help himself, his insistence that Zachary should return alone to the camp where the other members of the expedition waited.

'You wouldn't do that,' Wendy said. 'You knew he had no chance on his own.'

'I couldn't. Ben would never have left me.'

And then a blizzard had blown up, and Zachary had dug an ice cave for them, and the two friends had lain in it for days, sharing a sleeping bag, not knowing that the other section of their party was also in trouble further down the mountain and unable to come to their aid. And Ben had gradually become sicker and sicker, until he was drifting in and out of delirium, sometimes thinking he was in Christchurch with his wife and family, at other times reliving earlier adventures with his friend.

Zachary's narrative became more fluent, and Wendy's murmured interruptions less frequent. A couple of times when Zachary mentioned some incident that had come to Ben's mind in those last few hours, she said, 'I remember that...' or 'Yes, he was very happy that day...'

Zachary went on. 'He said, as though he couldn't quite believe it, that he wasn't going to make it this time, and he hoped that I'd come back some day and climb this mountain for him, get up there and show it could be done. And he said... "Tell Wendy I love her... always. And thank her for me."'

He had talked about the times he and Zachary had stood on high, lonely peaks together and felt the euphoria of gazing around with nothing between them and the clear sky, admiring the beauty of the world laid at their feet, feeling humbled and proud and immortal, at one with the splendour of creation.

'He said we were the lucky ones, because we knew how it felt to be touching the hand of God. He said he couldn't have asked for a better life, and he didn't regret any of it. Except leaving you, Wendy, and not seeing the girls grow up.' Zachary's voice faltered. 'And then he asked...for my hand. And he held it until...until it was all over.'

The tape went silent and hissed on unheeded to the end as Katrien sat with tears scalding her eyes and pouring down her cheeks.

CHAPTER ELEVEN

THE Snowfire company sent Katrien to the South Island for a photo shoot on Mount Cook. Afterwards she decided to travel to Christchurch and spend the weekend with Wendy, who had several times issued warm invitations to her to stay.

The two little girls were delightful children, who showed her a scrapbook of their father's exploits in the mountains, many of the photographs featuring 'Uncle Zach' as well.

'They seem to be getting over it,' Katrien ventured when the girls had gone to bed and she and Wendy were settled over cups of coffee. 'It will take longer for you.'

'It'll take a lifetime. But we made good memories together, and two terrific children. I'll never be sorry I married Ben.'

In awe and envy, Katrien wondered where such strength and serenity came from. 'Did you ever try to stop him climbing?'

Wendy looked appalled. 'Would you try to stop someone you loved from breathing?'

Katrien was silent for a while. 'You must have understood him very well.'

'Ben was a special person...different. Of course I worried about him. But people get killed crossing the street every day. One of our climbing friends died of leukaemia. Ben would have hated to go like that, in hospital and all hooked up to machines and tubes. None of us knows when someone we love will be snatched away from us. Today, tomorrow, in fifty years' time... What

was important was what we had now, what we did with
the time that was given to us, however long or short that
was going to be.'

'I...think I'm beginning to understand. When I listened to the tape Zachary made with you...to what he
and Ben talked about up there...it began to make some
kind of sense.' She had asked Wendy's permission to
reprint the tape almost verbatim in the book, and readily
received it. That chapter, the last, remained almost entirely intact in Zachary's own words, and was, she knew,
the most moving passage in the book. 'I was angry with
him,' she confessed. 'Because he was going back there,
and...'

'And it frightened you.' Wendy nodded. 'You're in
love with him, aren't you?'

'He doesn't care.'

'Katrien, it isn't that he doesn't care. I think...'

'Did he...talk about me?'

'A bit. Mostly he was very closed in, even before he
met you...ever since Ben died, really. As if there was
something on his mind that he couldn't shake.
Something more than grief.' A shadow darkened
Wendy's eyes. 'I tried to get him to tell me what bothered him, but I never did get to the bottom of it. Only I
think...you got to him somehow.'

'How?' Katrien asked blankly.

'I'm...not sure. It was a feeling I had. That he wanted
to protect you.'

The next day Wendy took Katrien and the children into
the city for lunch, and afterwards they strolled through
one of the parks that lined the banks of the Avon. The
river was slow and mostly shallow, although there were
places where currents eddied and the water was deep and
opaquely green. Tourists in punts poled by young men

in boater hats and blazers enjoyed leisurely rides along its winding length.

Stacey and Yasmin ran ahead with a couple of balloons that Katrien had bought for them from a street vendor. The five-year-old, Stacey, tripped on the path, letting her balloon go, and wailed with pain as Wendy picked her up. She had scraped her knee and the blood was running down her leg onto her white ankle sock. Her younger sister, a thumb in her mouth and her own balloon dangling from her hand, stood by silently watching.

Tissues from Wendy's bag failed to stop the flow, and Katrien dug in her own bag and found a handkerchief and handed it over.

'Thanks. Where's Yasmin?' Wendy asked sharply.

'She was here—' Katrien looked about them, and saw first the balloon the little girl was clutching, heading for the river bank, then ahead of her the one that her older sister had released, bouncing and floating towards the water. 'I'll get her.'

Even as she began to hurry across the lawn the freed balloon lifted and dropped into the river. And Yasmin, running as fast as her little legs would carry her, left the bank too and went hurtling in and under the water, a blur of pink and white being carried with frightening rapidity downstream, with her balloon bobbing on the surface.

Katrien, racing for the bank, heard Wendy scream, 'Yasmin!' She lost a shoe and paused to kick off the other one, running diagonally across the grass to bring her closer to the child, then without breaking her stride lifted her hands and took off in a long, shallow dive.

The water closed over her head and she knew a moment of sheer panic, then broke the surface and saw

Yasmin's frightened face just before the child went under again.

Her arms stroked quickly through the water. Dimly she heard more screams, and saw people running along the riverside, a man jump in from the opposite bank.

Then she touched wet fabric and a warm arm, and lifted the child, turning her on her back to keep her head out of the water.

Yasmin kicked and squirmed, shrieking, and a man's voice said, 'She's okay. Need some help there?'

They struggled to the bank, and then Wendy was there with Stacey in her arms, heedless of the blood staining her shirt and trousers, and gathering both the sobbing girls into her arms. She looked up at the young man who had leapt into the water and said, 'Thank you. Thank you so much. And Katrien—' She turned to her. 'I'll never be able to thank you both enough.'

Katrien sat shivering on the bank as people crowded about them. Someone miraculously produced a couple of towels, and Katrien gratefully used one, then handed it to the young man while Wendy briskly rubbed down her errant daughter with the other. Both girls had stopped crying, and now Yasmin seemed to be enjoying the attention the incident had garnered.

'What's your name?' Katrien asked her co-rescuer.

'Tom.' He grinned at her. 'Didn't really need me, did you? You're a better swimmer than I am.'

Swimmer, Katrien thought. I swam. She looked wonderingly at the water she'd so recently emerged from. It wasn't very deep really—an adult could probably stand in it. But she had needed to reach the child quickly.

Tom bent down to put a hand briefly on Yasmin's head, replied to something Wendy said, and walked away. Gradually the crowd dispersed, and Wendy bundled her wet and injured charges into the car and took them home.

Katrien flew back to Auckland, still with a sense of disbelief at what she'd done. The following week she went to the tepid pool, hired a private coach and admitted that she had a water phobia after a near-drowning as a child, but wanted to swim again.

It wasn't easy, but now she had the knowledge that when it was totally necessary she had gone into the water and swum with scarcely a thought. So surely she could do it again. And gradually she did. There was always a tiny kernel of caution that had been missing when she was young and full of the fearlessness of youth, but there came a day when she found herself nearly enjoying herself in the pool. It was a victory.

The news she'd been dreading hit the morning paper, the radio, and television. Zachary's expedition was in trouble in the Himalayas. The weather in the region had closed down; the team was overdue and had lost radio contact. Reporters talked in tones of carefully modulated gloom of a rerun of the previous tragedy. Archive film was resurrected of the team members, and Katrien was jolted by a picture of Zachary returning bleakly from the mountain the year before, to report the news of his friend's death.

She phoned Wendy and they talked quietly, trying to boost each other's spirits in the face of increasingly pessimistic reports. Katrien walked about with a lump of ice in her chest instead of a heart, her emotions numbed.

Then Wendy phoned her. 'Katrien—they're all right! Zachary's all right. They've radioed in, I've talked to him on a patch-through, and they're going to start walking out today.'

Katrien clapped a hand over the receiver because she was sobbing with relief.

'He made the summit—he did it. Ben would be so proud. Katrien? Are you okay?'

'Yes,' she whispered. 'Yes. Thank you, Wendy! Thank you, God!'

She put down the receiver, dropped her head into her hands and wept.

'I don't care what I'm supposed to be doing that day!' Katrien stormed into the phone. 'I'm *busy*.'

'Busy?' her agent stormed back at her. 'You have a contract!'

'Stuff the contract. That was a free day. They can't foist a new assignment on me at such short notice.'

'You never used to be temperamental,' Hattie said tartly. 'What on earth can be that important?'

'I'm going to the airport to meet...to meet the New Zealand Himałayan expedition, and nothing will stop me!'

There was a short silence. 'But that's exactly what the company wants you to do.'

'What?'

'The media will all be there. We want you there too, giving Zachary Ballantine a hero's welcome.'

'He won't want a hero's welcome.' In fact he'd be violently opposed to it.

'He'll be getting one anyway. You might as well make the most of the photo opportunity.'

'No!' If there was going to be a media event, stage-managed for the benefit of the press or the Snowfire company or both, she wanted no part of it. 'This is a private thing.'

'He's a public figure, Katrien. So are you. You can't

avoid it, you know. The whole country knows you two
are—'

'The whole country knows nothing!' Katrien snapped.

The agent sighed. 'Don't be difficult. The man's been
in the wilds of Katmandu—'

'Nepal. Katmandu is the capital city.'

'All right, Nepal—for months. They nearly died out
there, you know.'

Katrien shuddered. 'I know.'

'Well, after what he's been through, what man in his
right mind wouldn't want to come home to a warm smile
and a big, loving kiss from his—from the Snowfire girl?'

She had a sudden vision of Zachary in the darkened
passageway of her flat, his mouth on hers, his voice murmuring, 'I've dreamed of you…Snowfire girl.'

Had he dreamed of her when he was lost on that faraway mountain? Had he cared that he might never come
home, never see her again? Had he been hoping that
when she listened to his last tape she might understand
his compulsion?

And if he had, did she have a tiny, faint chance with
him after all?

Maybe she could live without him, as he could all too
obviously live without her. But wouldn't it amount to
only half a life? And could she persuade him that she
was capable of loving him without trying to bind him to
the earth when he belonged on Olympus with the gods?
That she loved him enough to allow his freedom?

'All right,' she said. 'I'll be there.'

They'd insisted that she wear the silver dress. The team
members were brought through Customs first, looking
tired and pale, a couple of them still bearded. Some were
pushing loaded luggage carts, others carried enormous
backpacks.

Zachary had a heavy day-old shadow on his cheeks, and when he saw Katrien he blinked and shook his head as though disbelieving his eyes. He took his hands from the luggage cart he was pushing, and it rolled a few feet on its own. He didn't seem to notice.

She walked towards him, quite unable to smile, and stood a couple of feet away. Flashbulbs popped, and he blinked again. A reporter thrust a microphone at him.

'Mr Ballantine, how does it feel to have finally conquered the peak where your friend died last year?'

Zachary pushed the mike away without looking at the woman. His eyes were on Katrien. 'What are you doing here?' He swayed, and she moved instinctively forward, putting her arms about him.

More cameras clicked, and lights flashed.

His arms came around her, and held her so that she could hardly breathe. She saw him close his eyes tightly and then his cheek was against hers and his incipient beard scratched her skin.

The Snowfire photographer said, 'Very nice. Now can we have a kiss? Come on, Katrien, turn this way a bit. Sir? Mr Ballantine?'

And Zachary lifted his head, his glazed eyes clearing. He saw the cameraman, and the other media people, and glanced down at Katrien's silver dress. His expression changed and his mouth went wry. 'I see. We'd better give them what you came for.'

His kiss was blindingly thorough, filled with a furious passion, and then he put her aside quite gently and said to the excited press people, 'Okay, folks. Enough for today. We're all very tired.' He looked round at the other men in the party, some of them being greeted effusively by families and girlfriends. 'Personally I want a clean hotel, a hot bath and a week's sleep.'

He went to retrieve his luggage trolley, and Katrien,

feeling suddenly tawdry in her spectacular dress, let her shoulders droop.

But why give up so easily? As he grasped the handle of the trolley she put her own hands on the metal bar and said, 'I'd hoped you'd come home with me.'

He must have seen the pleading in her eyes. The cameras and microphones were still trained on them. 'Is this part of the publicity stunt?' he asked wearily.

She could hardly blame him for thinking so, but she wished he trusted her more. 'We can talk there,' she urged. 'I need to talk to you, Zachary. Please. Let's at least get out of this…circus.'

He nodded. 'I heartily concur with that, anyway.'

Katrien took over from there, sending the photographer to summon the limo she'd arrived in as the Snowfire girl, and organising Zachary's baggage into the boot.

Sinking into the back seat with her, he looked slightly bemused as they left the airport. 'You have clout,' he murmured.

'A contract,' she retorted. 'That's why I had to meet you wearing this stupid dress. I was going to come anyway, but the Snowfire people wanted…'

'Publicity.' He shrugged. 'It's okay.'

'You don't mind?'

He shook his head. 'Not if you don't.' He leaned back, closing his eyes. She thought he was asleep.

When they got to the flat and the driver had helped him bring in his bags, she said, 'Make yourself at home. I'll change and then get us some coffee—and a snack?'

'Nothing for me,' he mumbled, looking longingly at the bed where he had spent so many nights. 'Thanks. A hot shower would be nice.'

'Of course. You know where the towels are.'

Hurrying into her room, she snatched off the silly

dress, throwing it across the bed and hauling out a sweat-shirt and jeans.

She hadn't heard the shower, and when she peeked into the spare room, Zachary was lying across the bed fast asleep.

He hardly stirred when she removed his boots. She pulled a cover over him and he mumbled and turned on his side. Smiling, she went into the sitting room to phone Wendy and tell the other woman he was home at last.

He stumbled into the bathroom hours later, when it was already dark outside. She heard the shower and closed the book she'd been reading while curled up in the two-seater. Guessing he'd be hungry, she went into the kitchen and made coffee and a generous plate of ham sandwiches.

Then he walked into the sitting room, barefoot and dressed in a tracksuit. He was freshly shaved and his hair damp.

'Did you wash my things?' he asked.

She'd washed and dried all the clothes in his pack while he slept on, oblivious, and placed them, neatly folded, on the chair by the bed.

'I hope you don't mind.'

'Mind?' He shook his head. 'I'm grateful.'

She smiled at him, and indicated the heaped plate on the low table alongside a pot of coffee and two mugs.

He ate and drank in silence, then leaned back in the chair opposite her and said, 'How did you know that's what I needed?'

'It's what I like after a long plane trip.'

'I love you,' he said.

Katrien nearly choked. 'What did you say?' She must have misheard.

'I love you.' As if he were saying, Pass the salt, or, What a nice day.

'Wh-when did you decide that?' she demanded, feeling peculiarly cheated. Was this the result of being overdue on the mountain? Maybe there was something to be said for it after all.

Zachary gave her a crooked little smile. 'I've always known it. Only I couldn't tell you before. Not until I'd climbed that bastard.'

Outraged, Katrien almost screeched at him. 'Why the hell not?'

He shrugged, looking strangely embarrassed, and she worked it out for herself. 'You thought I'd try to stop you,' she said. 'You didn't want to give me a…a weapon to make you stop.' She paused, fighting anger that she realised was probably unfair, and reluctantly admitted, 'You were right. I would have tried…because I didn't understand.'

'I was afraid to take that risk.'

'I do understand now,' she said hesitantly. 'I think.'

He raised his brows at her in disbelieving silence.

'At least, enough to promise you I won't ever try to stop you.'

'You won't?' His smile grew, but there was something decidedly odd about it.

'All I want is for you to be happy,' she told him. 'And if that means spending half your life in the mountains, that's what you must do.'

'And you won't go out of your mind with worry?'

Katrien swallowed. Of course she would, but whether they were together or not didn't make any difference to the thousand deaths she would die every time she knew he was climbing. 'I'll survive,' she said bravely. If only you do.

He stood up and came over to her, taking her hands

and drawing her to her feet, facing him. 'Will you marry me, Snowfire girl?'

She stopped breathing for an instant. 'Yes,' she whispered, accepting the waiting, and the fear, and the very real possibility of a pain she couldn't even imagine, that she'd had only a taste of these last few weeks.

'And have my children?'

There was the briefest hesitation while she thought of Ben Storey's two bright-eyed little girls proudly showing her the scrapbook of their father. 'Yes.'

'Then I don't need to climb any more mountains,' Zachary said.

Her eyes widened. 'You're not—you can't give it up! I won't let you do it—not for me!'

He looked down at the hands he was still holding. 'How about for me?' he asked her quietly.

'But…it's your life…climbing.' Worry hushed her voice. 'You've never wanted to do anything else—'

'Wrong. Once I wanted to be a champion skier. Then I wanted to be a scientist. That's what I am, a scientist with an interest in mountains. Ben was the one who had the mystical feeling for them. Together we made a good team.'

'But…'

'He could never have given up climbing. It was a part of what he was. Wendy knew that, and so did I. I shared a lot of unforgettable moments with him, moments I'll treasure for the rest of my life, but now he's gone, and it's never going to be like that again.'

Hope beat heavily in her heart. 'You've always climbed. How will you live without it?'

'I've done what Ben asked me to. And what I…what I had to do for my own self-respect.'

'Self-respect?'

He was holding her hands tightly. 'There's something

I need to tell you...something I haven't told anyone.' He paused for a deliberate, deepened breath. 'I told you that you'd helped me more than you knew when you went climbing with me on Ruapehu—but you didn't know what I meant.'

'I couldn't see how...'

'After Ben's death I suffered...well, I guess you'd call it a crisis of confidence. He and I had the utmost trust in each other, but he was the real genius in the mountains. He would take risks that would have been disastrous for most people and pull them off. He loved the mountains and they seemed to love him back. He understood them so well, intuitively. I suppose I almost believed...and I think he felt like it...that he was in some sense immortal.'

'No one is immortal.'

'No.' He looked down at their joined hands. 'Well, I learned that lesson when Ben was killed. If he couldn't survive, I felt that...I must be next. It wasn't just that the magic had gone. All my own ability and experience seemed to have no relevance any more. For the first time I was truly, deathly afraid.'

Her mouth parted in astonishment. She remembered his pallor when he'd taken her climbing. He'd been sweating even though she knew he was much fitter than she was. At the time she'd thought nothing of it. That his physical condition was born of a very real fear had never crossed her mind.

He said, 'I was so scared I had to force myself to start again from where I'd begun as a kid, first skiing, then working up to cross-country, and finally climbing.' He looked at her worriedly. 'I should never have taken you with me that day. It was criminally irresponsible. If I'd dipped out then, left you in the lurch...'

She brushed that aside as unthinkable. She knew he

would never have done that, never left her in danger no matter what it cost him. 'But it helped?'

'Oh, yes. I had to think about you, not myself. And your trust in me...well, I had to live up to that, so that day I proved I could do it. The next time I tried something harder, and I knew that technically I was okay. But...I also knew deep down that I was a shivering coward, not the hero you persisted in calling me, in seeing me as. Nothing like it.'

'Zachary.' She touched his cheek, making him look at her. 'You went back to the Himalayas to prove you weren't afraid?'

'I went in the certainty that I was going to die. That I'd never make it back alive.'

Katrien gasped. 'And yet you still...' Words failed her.

'What a man's gotta do and all that crazy macho stuff. I felt I couldn't face you...or myself...knowing that I had lost any courage I might once have had.'

'You are not a coward!'

He grimaced in wry self-mockery. 'No? That last night—why do you think I did what I swore I was never going to do...?'

'You made love to me.'

'I've never been so ashamed in all my life.'

'Ashamed!' Katrien stared indignantly.

'I'd been telling myself I had no right to take your love and leave you to grieve for me. I'd seen what happened to the women my friends left behind. To Wendy. She's strong and she puts a brave face on it for the girls, and for Ben's parents. Only once, when I was staying with her...she let go.' He took a deep breath, his eyes darkening. 'I have never seen such pain.' His voice shook. 'I *never* wanted to put any woman through that on my behalf. Especially you. I knew I'd fallen completely, irrevocably in love with you—it happened so fast I had no time to put up defences against it.'

'You made a pretty good pretence of it, then. It convinced me.'

'I was as convincing as I knew how. I…felt that you were falling for me. But I thought…as long as I didn't let things go too far you'd be all right. Whatever happened to me, you'd get over it. Only I slipped badly… twice.'

'I know now why you were so repelled when I called you my hero.'

'Repelled?' He shook his head. 'Guilty, shocked, ashamed. It certainly brought me up with a bump, made me remember I had no right to involve myself with you, no matter that I tried to buy your argument that you were entitled to make your own decision. I told myself that if you were content with half a loaf it was okay. What you didn't know was that you were getting half a man.'

'I never heard such arrant nonsense!' Katrien said roundly. She felt like shaking him. 'Being afraid to climb a peak that killed your best friend shows a lot of common sense, if you ask me! You men are so…so…'

'Male?' He smiled at her.

'Stupid is the word that comes to mind, actually.'

'Is that so?' His eyes gleamed at her. Then he laughed as if she'd relieved his mind.

'Are you serious about giving up?'

'Deadly serious. If you're going to marry me I don't want to spend half my life away from you.'

'What will you do?'

'I'll find something. I have had offers from time to time, of jobs in science, or teaching mountain safety or outdoor skills. There's a job in Search and Rescue administration that I've heard about…'

She put her arms about him, vastly relieved that he

felt so solid and warm and definitely real. 'I'm so glad you didn't die on that mountain.'

'You kept me alive.'

'Me?'

'I couldn't help thinking of that night we spent together before I left, and I knew that if I just made it this one more time I could give it all up and come home to you. When I saw you at the airport I couldn't believe my eyes. I was exhausted and jet-lagged and I thought I must be seeing things. Especially since you were wearing that dress...it seemed so unlikely.'

'You were angry because you thought it was just a publicity stunt for Snowfire.'

'Momentarily,' he agreed. 'It was a bit of a let-down after I'd just convinced myself you were there because you couldn't keep away.'

'I was. I argued with my agent, threatened to breach my contract to go and meet you. Then she said the company wanted me to anyway so I didn't have a leg to stand on.'

'I'm still not sure this is real,' he said soberly. 'Maybe I'm asleep on the plane. Or in an ice cave on the mountain. Maybe I'm dreaming again. I dreamed of you so often.'

'Shall I kiss you awake?' She smiled at him, and kissed his mouth, and felt his response.

'Do that again,' he muttered, his eyes still closed as she drew away.

Katrien did it again, slow and delicious, and he opened his eyes and said, 'It's a dream, but don't wake me up.'

'If it's a dream,' she said, smiling, kissing his chin, 'why aren't you in bed?'

'Good question,' he murmured, and swung her up into

his arms, carrying her from the room. 'Which one shall it be?'

'I don't care,' she said, her eyes shining with longing and sweet anticipation, 'as long as it's one I can share with the hero of my dreams.'

'That's me,' he said, smiling down at her with all the confidence in the world.

'Yes,' Katrien said softly. 'Yes, it is. It was always you.'

AMERICAN ♦ ROMANCE®

Invites *you* to experience the most upbeat, lively romances around!

Every month, we bring you four strong, sexy men, and four women who know what they want—and go all out to get it.

We'll take you from the places you know to the places you've dreamed of. Live the love of a lifetime!

American Romance—

Love it! Live it!

Makes any time special ™

Visit us at www.romance.net.

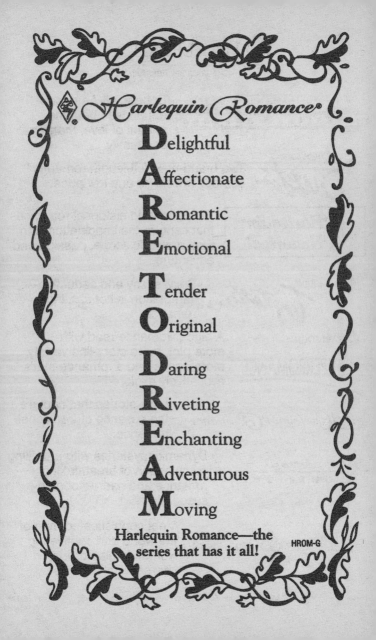

Harlequin Romance®

Delightful
Affectionate
Romantic
Emotional
Tender
Original
Daring
Riveting
Enchanting
Adventurous
Moving

Harlequin Romance—the
series that has it all!

HROM-G

Harlequin® Historical

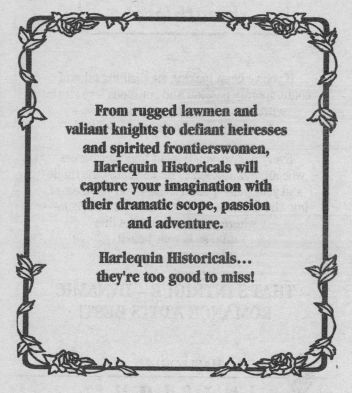

From rugged lawmen and
valiant knights to defiant heiresses
and spirited frontierswomen,
Harlequin Historicals will
capture your imagination with
their dramatic scope, passion
and adventure.

Harlequin Historicals…
they're too good to miss!

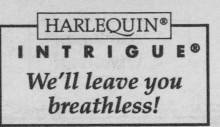